OWNING IT

First published in the UK in 2025 by Faber and Faber Limited,
The Bindery, 51 Hatton Garden, London, EC1N 8HN
faber.co.uk

Typeset in Mr Eaves Mod OT by Faber
This font has been specially chosen to support reading
Printed and bound by CPI Group (UK) Ltd, Croydon, CR0 4YY

A CIP record for this book is available from the British Library

ISBN 978–0–571–38002–2

FSC
www.fsc.org

MIX
Paper | Supporting
responsible forestry
FSC® C013604

Printed and bound in the UK on FSC® certified paper in line with our continuing
commitment to ethical business practices, sustainability and the environment.
For further information see faber.co.uk/environmental-policy

Our authorised representative in the EU for product safety is
Easy Access System Europe, Mustamäe tee 50, 10621 Tallinn, Estonia
gpsr.requests@easproject.com

2 4 6 8 10 9 7 5 3 1

For this generation of disabled kids (and future ones, too!). Here are the words we wish we'd owned when we were your age. We hope you find comfort, laughter, joy and solidarity here.

OWNING IT

Edited by

Jen Campbell, James Catchpole and Lucy Catchpole

Illustrated by

Sophie Kamlish

Stories from

Ali Abbas, Polly Atkin, Imani Barbarin, Jen Campbell, James Catchpole, Christa Couture, Carly Findlay, M. Leona Godin, Eugene Grant, Jan Grue, Matilda Feyiṣayọ Ibini, Ilya Kaminsky, Sora J. Kasuga, Jessica Kellgren-Fozard, Elle McNicoll, Daniel Sluman, Nina Tame, Rebekah Taussig, Steven Verdile, Alex Wegman, Ashley Harris Whaley and Kendra Winchester.

faber

Contents

Dear reader,

This is the book we wish we'd had when we were young.

As disabled children, we didn't see many people like us in the books we read or the films we watched. And, when we did, we usually wished we hadn't! If they were the good guys, they were inspirational people whose disability was their 'superpower'. If they were the bad guys, their disability was part of their evilness – like Captain Hook – which was annoying. And boring.

Because, really, disability isn't like that, is it? Disability is a normal part of everyday life. Did you know that about a quarter of people are disabled?[1] That's a lot of people! And we think books and films should show that, too: how normal it is to be disabled.

Perhaps you are disabled yourself, or you know someone who is? You probably know someone who will be, one day. Some people are born disabled, and some become disabled later in life. Of the three of us editing this book, two of us – James and Jen – were born disabled, and one of us – Lucy – became disabled later.

---

1   According to UK government disability statistics, published August 2023.

There are so many ways of being disabled, and so many ways of feeling about it, too. That's something we wanted to show and celebrate in this book. Each chapter is written by a different writer, and each writer was once a disabled child. This book is not a perfect cross section of the disabled community, though we did our best to find writers with as wide a range of disabilities and backgrounds as possible.[2]

We asked these writers to tell us about a memory from their childhood – something joyful or challenging or funny. In this book, you're going to read about Jan skating across the Norwegian ice in his wheelchair, Matilda stargazing with her mum in Nigeria, and James leaving his leg at home (yes, really!). However, while people have such different bodies and lead such different lives, the things they need and want and wish for are often similar, so this book celebrates that as well.

We can't change our disabilities. But we can own them. That's what the title of this book means. If you're disabled and you don't feel like you're owning it right now, that's OK. Hang in there. Growing up with a disability isn't easy, sometimes because of our own

---

2   We work as writers and publishing people in the UK, and we've reached out to writers, first and foremost. Our pool of contributors cannot help but reflect this.

bodies and sometimes because of the world around us. Many of us were made to feel ashamed of our disabilities when we were young. Many of us weren't given the words to talk about that part of ourselves, so we could be proud to be disabled and find strength in our togetherness.

Our hope is that you find the strength and the pride and the words you need. Some of them might even be in this book.

All our love,

Jen, James and Lucy

Teddy Bear Island

by Rebekah Taussig

United States

The evening of Family Fun Night at Carousel Park, I was nervous. An entire evening of unstructured play in a giant indoor amusement park with all the kids in our elementary school, plus their families, didn't really sound like a 'fun' night to me. I'd just started fifth grade, I was ten, and it wasn't going great. My class was crowded with twelve rowdy boys and five girls who held hands with those boys at recess and wore shirts with the words 'Gap' and 'Old Navy' and 'Limited' printed on the fronts.

My family couldn't afford to shop for clothes in stores like these. We went thrift shopping twice a year, when I would scour the aisles for shirts with the most expensive brands printed across the front. I thought maybe this would trick people into believing I was the same as them.

More than almost anything in the world, I wanted to fit in. It was more important than figuring out long division or being kind or drawing something that made me proud. The only problem with this goal was that 'fitting in' wasn't something I could really do. At least, not in the way I'd imagined it. I'd been using a hot pink wheelchair to get around since I was six. I wore leg braces that were strapped against my shins with brown Velcro. I used the bathroom in the nurse's office, while everyone else used the stalls. Every single person in my fifth-grade class was different in some ways and the same in others, but everyone noticed my differences right away, and there wasn't much I could do to hide them.

It's not that the kids at my school were mean to me. People didn't make fun of me or call me names. But I found myself alone a lot – sitting on the edge of the playground or relegated to the very end of the lunch table (the only spot my wheelchair could scoot under). Every once in a while, I was even a trend. For a week or so, the kids in my class would clamour to be my 'helper'. It wasn't an official title, but a self-appointed role. They'd get in line to push me to recess or carry my lunch tray. It wasn't a literal line, but a list I stored in my desk to make sure I kept it fair – if someone wanted a turn, they had to wait until everyone else on the list got a chance. I thought it should feel good – isn't it nice when people want to be around you? Instead, I felt a little more like the class hamster than anyone's friend. An object of affection, but not an equal.

That feeling of separation only grew when, a few weeks before fifth grade started, I was one of six nominated for our city's Outstanding Community Kid Award. I was ten years old. The local newspapers covered the story, recounting my life of 'painful treatments and surgeries', concluding, 'her courage inspires others to have faith and hope.' My mom snipped the articles out of the newspaper and sealed each behind the magnetic paper of my photo album, a black-and-white preservation of Rebekah Taussig, unconquerable fifth grader.

The gap between me and the kids around me felt wide. I lived on an island all of my own, and I didn't know how to build a bridge. So, I begged my mom to take me shopping in one of the expensive stores. My mom relented. I was allowed to pick out one top and one bottom for the new school year, despite the fact she really didn't have the money for either.

On Family Fun Night, I put on my brand-new khaki corduroy overalls and a long-sleeved striped top. It was a sweltering choice for that humid September, but wearing them made me feel a little bit like I belonged.

Carousel Park was supposed to be a hub for family entertainment, sprawled across the basement of a mostly abandoned mall. My parents dropped me off by the doors, and I pushed myself across the sidewalk in the bright heat of the late summer evening hours, sweat trickling down my neck. What games would I be able to play? Would anyone want to hang out with me? Or would they let me tag along out of pity? How would I know the difference?

Inside, my eyes adjusted to the dim party-scape. I pushed myself across the thick carpet covered in bright geometric shapes and tried to keep track of all the lights flashing across arcade games and small rides. Every minute I spent alone was a slow hour of torture. I felt people's eyes on me. Imagined? Real? Did it matter? I just needed to find a group of humans who wouldn't be annoyed by my presence. I tried to twist my mouth into a casual smile and kept rolling. Finally, I collided with a group of boys from my class playing an arcade game called Skee-Ball. The game was low to the ground, almost the perfect height for a girl in a wheelchair to throw a small ball and see what happens.

I didn't know these boys very well. There was the boy with a billion freckles who drew cartoons in his notebook during recess; the boy who mumbled nervously when he did math problems on the board and always got them wrong; the boy who wore a Pokémon sweatshirt every other day – one that had started out white but turned pale pink because of what I could only assume was a laundry accident. I quietly approached, stopping a couple of feet from their circle, hoping I could seamlessly join their group without making waves. They smiled in my direction, but no one said anything to me.

Chad, the kid wearing the pale pink Pokémon shirt, threw the little skee ball towards the hoops and missed the bullseye by a mile. He threw up his hands dramatically, making a show of his misfortune: 'I was so close!' I thought about making a joke, like – 'So close – to the gutter!' – but suddenly my tongue felt very big, and my throat felt very tight. This was my moment to wave a friendly flag! I swallowed several times, but it didn't help. I couldn't will myself to speak. And suddenly, in the silence, a voice broke through – 'Rebekah, you take a turn!' Chad held out a small ball to me.

The invitation felt like sunshine cutting through a heavy cloud, a brief quieting of a violent windstorm, the rainbow after the flood. I didn't know what I'd done to deserve this miraculous invitation, but I grabbed hold of it with both hands. 'Yeah, OK,' I said, holding the ball and pushing myself into just the right position to throw.

That night, we were the awkward bunch – a group of outsiders clinging to each other in the blinking beeping jungle, travelling from Skee-Ball to air hockey to the mini basketball hoops as one bubble. Together in this chaotic, flashing wilderness we were foragers on an adventure, surviving only because we'd joined forces. We started collecting our tickets and wondered together if pooling our resources would mean we could get something extra cool. But first, we wanted to go on the biggest ride on the floor – the Flying Dragon.

As I sat in the plastic car – one part of this wild, mechanical beast whipping across the tracks – I felt like I was actually soaring through outer space, passing friendly alien spaceships, glittering stars and big bright moons, my pals beside and behind me. My cheeks ached from smiling. As I pulled myself out of the ride and back into my wheelchair waiting by the entrance, one of the managers approached me. Had I broken some kind of rule? Maybe they didn't want kids who used wheelchairs on this ride?

The man pulled his trouser legs up a couple of inches and crouched low so his eyes were level with mine, his forearms resting on his thighs. 'Hi, Rebekah!' he said, loud enough to be heard above the noise of games and noisy kids. 'We heard about your "inspirational kid award", and we just wanted to be able to do something special for you.' He had such a giant, expectant grin on his face.

I looked back at my new-found group of friends. They stood in a cluster, watching me and the man from a few feet back, unsure what to do. I wasn't terribly interested in the special thing this man had in store for me. At the same time, I didn't want to take away the good feeling he had about giving it to me, and I didn't want my friends to have to wait for me either.

'You guys go ahead,' I said. 'I'll catch up with you.'

I followed the man towards the middle of the arcade where the bright booth full of prizes radiated rewards: snap bracelets, whoopee cushions, neon plastic yo-yos, inflatable penguins, miniature basketballs, all kinds of candy.

'Do you see those bears on the very top shelf?' he asked, leaning down to talk directly in my ear. I pulled back and smiled, looking up at a row of giant bears I hadn't noticed. Each bear was dressed in a different outfit and sat about three feet tall. They were enormous and childish. I nodded to the man.

'Those are our very biggest prizes, and we would like to give one to you,' he said, beaming.

I didn't have to ask the man why. Despite the fact that I hadn't earned more than thirteen tickets the whole night, I already knew. It was the same reason I'd been given the Outstanding Community Kid Award. For inspiring everyone with my 'painful treatments and surgeries' – my courage to show up in my wheelchair.

I was also almost eleven. If I was going to be given something for nothing, I'd much rather a box of Skittles or one of the cheap beaded bracelets. Still, the man in front of me looked excruciatingly proud of himself. So, I turned to him.

'Wow! That's so nice of you! Thank you, **thank you**!' I gushed. I picked the one with the wire spectacles and blue overalls. Even then, I knew the intent behind this exercise was to make me feel special. I also knew it left me feeling lonely and uncomfortable, but I couldn't have told you why. It took me much longer to realise that I didn't actually want to feel special. Or, at least, not special for my wheelchair and leg braces. I wanted to feel something else – seen, known, accepted, connected – something.

I didn't find my way back to my group of misfit pals that night. I don't remember why. Maybe because I could barely see over the giant stuffed animal in my lap? Maybe I just found my parents and told them I was ready to go home? Either way, the spell was broken.

The morning after Carousel Park, there was a picture of me in the local newspaper, beaming like a star, holding a teddy bear almost as big as me in my lap. The caption described the large turnout to Family Fun Night, listing all the fun activities of the night, including the presentation of a giant teddy bear to the girl who won a 'most inspirational kid' award. The article concludes, 'Many kids thought the highlight of the night was singing to the karaoke machine and dancing to the Macarena!' I must have missed that part of the festivities.

When I saw the group of boys again at school, it was like our night together had never happened. We looked at the floor and returned to our little islands. My mom helped me put the teddy bear up on the highest shelf of my closet. I didn't know what else to do with it.

For seven years, that teddy bear sat in my closet. It sat there while I struggled through and finally finished fifth grade. It sat there as I started middle-school with the worst haircut in human history. It sat there as I slowly started to realise that maybe other people are also looking for a way to belong – and maybe being the same as everyone else isn't the same as belonging. It sat there as I slowly started to take pride in quirky thrift store finds, filling up my closet with one-of-a-kind retro graphic tees and brightly coloured sneakers. And it was still sitting there when I became friends with Bertie and Marie.

Bertie was quiet with a big wide smile and pink cheeks that flushed even pinker when she was flustered. We both played flute in the seventh-grade band, when we were twelve, and whenever I found myself sitting quietly to the side as people filed loudly and clumsily into or out of the band room, Bertie was always there too. We'd roll our eyes together at the chaos and wait for the dust to settle before making any moves. We also went to the same church, which is where we met Marie, a girl with long dark hair and bangs cut just above her glasses. Marie was never the loudest kid in the room, but the first time I invited her over to my house we watched *The*

Princess Bride on a tiny TV in my brother's bedroom and laughed so hard we collapsed on the floor in tears. And when the three of us were together, we were as busy and silly as three baby squirrels jumping from branch to telephone wire to rooftop.

For most of my childhood, my wheelchair felt like a sort of wall between me and my peers. Sometimes it led to a literal barrier of separation – a flight of stairs, an inaccessible playground or a lunch table that didn't work well with my wheelchair. Other times it was harder to pin down. People treated me differently, like they were afraid – if they got too close, played freely or said the wrong thing, I might break. Or maybe I expected them to treat me differently and put the wall up myself before they had the chance. Maybe it was a little bit of both. Either way, I didn't want to be anyone's class pet – cute and novel until I became a chore – and I didn't need anyone trying to make me feel special. I just wanted real friends. I couldn't even imagine what that would look like until I found it.

Bertie and Marie learned how to load my wheelchair on and off the yellow school bus and weren't afraid to scuff it up. When we arrived somewhere my wheelchair couldn't easily glide, one of them would stoop beside me and I would climb on her back. Natural. Easy. It felt more like playing around than being helped. Which is probably what it looked like, too. One morning, soon after Bertie turned seventeen and got her driver's licence, we made a quick trip to the gas station for Slurpees. We left my chair in her driveway, and when we arrived at the shop I hopped on Marie's back. As soon as we walked through the front doors, the shop clerk shouted at us, 'None of that roughhousing in here!' We all feigned innocence. Bertie said, 'She's **paralysed**,' her eyes accusatory and dramatic. He looked sceptical. Also embarrassed. 'Well, be careful,' he mumbled, eyeing us as we pranced down the aisles, giggling.

Everything we did, we did big. Make some treats for the church bake sale? Let's spend the entire weekend making fifteen pies, six gallons of puppy chow and five trays of Rice Krispie treats! Celebrate one of our birthdays? Let's plan an elaborate murder-mystery party, complete with clue books and a whole cast of characters performing all the parts! Go thrift shopping? Let's fill a van with our friends and take a mini road trip to another town where we'll spend the entire day trying on outfits for each other! Play a midnight practical joke? None of this default toilet-papering someone's yard – let's buy rolls of plastic wrap and cocoon an entire car! Which is exactly how we found ourselves in a back-and-forth war of pranks with the boys from our church.

One weekend, the three of us sat in my bedroom coming up with ideas. We needed the perfect prank – the kind the average prankster hadn't dreamed of, but when they saw it, they'd know: genius. Should we sprinkle birdseed all over their yards so they'd wake up to a million crows feasting? Something with instant potatoes, that would lie in wait until it rained, when the yard would explode into a gooey mess? Everything felt too elaborate or mean. We looked around my room for ideas – a closet full of pictures, my old flute, and there at the top, tucked away for safe-keeping, a row of old stuffed animals from years past – a raggedy lamb named 'Lucy' I used to take with me to chemotherapy treatments, the pink bunny with the stuffing falling out of one foot, and, of course, the giant teddy bear with the wire spectacles. It was probably the first time a human hand had touched him in years. His fur was dusty.

We grabbed as many as we could and loaded them into Bertie's car, laughing maniacally into the night. We turned down our music when we arrived at the house where all the boys were staying that night, their cars parked in the driveway. I climbed onto Bertie's back, holding stuffed animals in each hand. Marie was close behind, her arms full. We stifled our giggles as we quietly opened one of the car doors and stuffed as many animals as we could under the strap of each seat belt.

Finally, we turned to our crown jewel – the giant teddy bear with the wire spectacles. He'd arrived on my lap seven years before, an unwanted, awkward gift. For years, the sight of him brought a tiny weight to my gut – a mixture of embarrassment from being made into a spectacle and rage from feeling so powerless to opt out or say no. But that night, as we tucked him in the driver's seat, paws reaching for the steering wheel, seat belt pulled across his blue overalls, the story of me and this bear shifted. Suddenly, it felt ridiculous. Hilarious. Feather light. I couldn't stop laughing at this giant bear with a belly full of fluff driving a teenage boy's car. I pictured the guys coming out of their house the next morning, so cool and above it all, only to be met with a child's oversized bear in overalls. I could hardly breathe with the giddy power of being the authors of such a nonsensical scene. I didn't know it right then, but that night, I took a story I'd been given against my will, and, with the help of my friends, I wrote a new one.

We bolted back to Bertie's car and drove into the night with the windows down, blasting our mix CD of Chicago's greatest hits. Free and silly and together.

I learned at a young age that my wheelchair and leg braces prompted a lot of reactions in people – pity, fear, a desire to help. I think that's where the special awards and lunchroom helpers and giant teddy bear came from. But being with Bertie and Marie felt different. While there would always be parts of my life they couldn't understand first-hand, they saw me – my dramatic lip-synching, my monochromatic, mixed-print, thrifted outfits, my disability, my obsessive baking ambitions – and wanted to be my friend. My body wove seamlessly, lightly, playfully into our rhythms, just like anything else. I didn't need a giant teddy bear on my island. I wanted an island with a bridge. And the three of us laid down so many bridges between our cluster of islands we built our own kingdom where we could prance back and forth, under and over – a universe all our own.

Faking It

by James Catchpole

United Kingdom

People always want to know what happened to my leg.
They did when I was a kid, and they still do now that I'm
forty-something. So I'm going to tell you.

It's a good story. Ready?

My leg never really felt like part of me, and this feeling
grew over time, so that, by the end of primary school, I'd
started to feel I'd be better off without it. And soon after
I started secondary school, I knew it was time for action.
So, off came the leg.

My parents were a little anxious, it must be said. They
worried for my health. But I reckoned it was my decision
at that point – I was thirteen after all – and they couldn't
really stop me. I just did it myself one morning before
school: I left my leg there, on the bedroom floor, and off
I went.

Best decision I ever made.

I hope you've worked out by now that I'm talking about

my fake leg. If not, then that last scene must have looked kind of dramatic in your head. Was it . . . messy? Sorry. I can tell you now, no home-surgery involved. No one had to shampoo the carpet.

The leg I ditched at thirteen was the false one. That's what we called it: my false leg. And that's how it felt to me, by that stage: like a fake. A counterfeit.

I'm a single-leg, through-hip amp – pretty much always have been. The first part of that is medical-speak for 'one leg, all off'; the last part is amp-speak for 'amputee'. And 'amputee' just means you're down a leg or arm, or two.

As a leg amputee, from the time I could stand up, I'd been given a prosthesis – a false leg – to walk on. If that brings to mind those dashing Paralympians, charging round a running track on futuristic blades, then do by all means enjoy that thought. I do. Those guys are excellent. But that was never an option, and not just because it was A Long Time Ago.

To run with a blade, you need part of a real leg to attach it to. Just a few inches of leg will do. But being a through-hip amp means there's nothing below your bum. And you can't attach a running blade to your bum.

Well, you probably can, but not in any useful way. No, a through-hip prosthesis doesn't really conjure the word 'dashing'. It's a modified bucket-and-stick job. You sit in the bucket and walk on the stick. I say 'walk', but it's more of a lurch, really – you know, like Lurch, from *The Addams Family*.

To be fair to the prosthetists, they did their best and the modifications were clever. There was a rubbery foot-shaped foot to give you some balance and spring. And there were joints: a 'free hip' to allow the leg to swing forwards independently of the rest of you, which did make things just a little less lurchy; and for the very daring, a 'free knee', 'for the smoothest, most natural walk'.

I liked the idea of a free knee, because it rhymed, which made it sound like a political slogan, and who doesn't like the idea of freedom, even for knees, which work so hard after all. But I never mastered it. There was a price to be paid for walking more smoothly. To walk with a free knee, you needed to walk slowly and evenly. And what kid wants to walk slowly and evenly? I tried rushing and collapsing for a bit, then gave up on the free knee, and went back to rushing and lurching. Sorry, knee.

You may not know this, but they weigh a bit, through-hip false legs. Especially grown-up ones. These days, if I leave mine standing in front of the snack cupboard, my youngest daughter can just about drag it clear so she can reach her crisps after nursery. She's almost four, though, and powered by crisp-lust. A year ago when she tried moving my leg, she tended to get squished.

When I was little, like her, I don't remember the leg feeling heavy. I used to rush around the playground on it happily enough. The action must have been a kind of rapid lurching – a tiny, utterly unselfconscious gallop. In fact, I can remember demonstrating my fastest gallop to the class at six or seven, and charging headlong into a stack of chairs.

There's a report from the headmaster of the school I joined at eight, which says much the same. He's reassuring my parents that I'm 'tearing around the playground' with everyone else. And I think that was true enough.

By the time I finished at that school five years later, I wasn't tearing around, though. They make bigger legs for you as you grow, and the proportions stay the same. But somehow, what felt easy enough at eight no longer felt so easy at twelve. By then, I'd started to feel the leg was a weight I was dragging along with me – like an anchor. I can't say why, exactly, but as I got bigger, the lurching got slower and harder – and sorer, too.

I'd also become more aware of how different my false leg made me from everybody else. Having one leg wasn't a problem. Funnily enough, I'd always been fine with that. No, it was the false leg that was giving me doubts. It was hard to see at the time, but we'd grown apart, the leg and I. We just wanted different things. And frankly, I'd started to question its worldview.

Because here's the other thing, besides the weight and the lurching. My false leg had impossible dreams. It wanted to be a real leg. You could tell, because they'd covered the stick bit in squishy, flesh-coloured foam and sculpted it in the shape of a real leg. It looked like they'd hacked a leg off some kid and stuffed it in one half of my posh granny's tights. They'd covered the bucket bit in thin, flesh-coloured rubber, too, and that just looked, well, like half a bum. With air holes.

I wasn't buying it. Nobody was going to see me in my pants and say, 'Why, that kid has two almost-identical legs! And he's wearing tights! But only on one of them! And he appears to have airholes drilled across half of his bum . . . But other than that, identical!'

Nevertheless, my false leg **was** supposed to pass as a real leg. It was designed not to be seen, but to be hidden. It was supposed to be worn under clothes. The sculpted foam was there to nicely fill a trouser. The flesh colour was in case I wanted to wear shorts, I suppose (or flash my bum at someone **very quickly**). And as long as I put it on every morning, preferably under long trousers, and walked with it slowly and evenly, on a free knee, and didn't take it off until I was home again, then no one would need to know the awful truth of my one-leggedness.

And what a relief that would be! Not just for me, you understand, but for anyone who might have been disturbed or discomfited by the sight of me . . .

I should say, no one gave me that message explicitly – not that I remember, anyway – but that was the message that seemed to be implied by the whole process of limb-fitting: **you'll probably want to hide that as best you can, so as to fit in**.

Maybe I shouldn't be surprised by this. My false leg was being fitted in the 1980s – a time as close to the Second World War as it is to now. In fact, the man who made my first legs had looked after fighter-pilot ace Douglas Bader, who had famously fought the Nazis on a pair of falsies. You can see him in the biopic *Reach for the Sky*, learning to walk again after his flying accident, all glorious stiff upper lip and pipe smoke.

I imagine a dignified lurch and a walking stick were quite the badge of honour back then, along with military medals and marrying your nurse. But what I was finding, forty years on, was that false legs that pretended to be real legs just confused people.

I still got the questions, like, 'Why do you walk funny?' But when I told the other kids, 'It's a false leg,' they tended to feel, well, tricked. Either they believed me, and realised I'd been tricking them into thinking I had two normal legs, or they thought I was **still** tricking them by **pretending** one of my legs was fake. I have a memory of keeping a set of compasses in my pocket – they had a sharp steel tip for digging into paper – so that I could make a show of stabbing my right leg, just to convince people it was fake: one conjuring trick to disprove another!

The trickiest thing about the trick, though, is that you can end up accepting the idea behind it: that it's best for everyone – for you and for others – if you don't show anyone who you really are. And that idea leads to **all kinds** of difficulties.

What about school sports? All week, you drag this leg-shaped anchor around, this conjuring trick to hide your difference. And then twice a week, when sport comes along, you go into a changing room with all the other kids in your class and pull back the curtain to let daylight in on the magic. Well, actually it's a little more awkward than pulling back a curtain:

1. Belt open, trousers down to knees to reveal socket.
2. Undo Velcro straps around socket, ease bum out of socket and sit down, leaving leg standing.
3. Take shoe and trouser leg off real leg, pull trousers back over false leg and lean it against bench. Then for sports involving the leg . . .
4. Turn the leg upside down and lever the shoe off (with a 'shoehorn' where needed), before undressing it and redressing it in shorts and a sports shoe.
5. Put shorts over real foot, add sporting footwear, stand up, re-attach leg, pull up shorts.

Needless to say, all the other kids are out on the sports pitch already, and by the time you've trudged out there on the leg, the lesson is mercifully half-done.

For sports where the leg would get in the way (like gymnastics) or drown you (like swimming), getting changed is a little quicker – you can stop after Step 3. But then you have to step out of the changing room as your true, one-legged self in the full light of day . . . So what was the point in faking it the rest of the time?

I was very lucky with my school: no one teased me. Well, one kid did, just once, and only in passing in an exploratory kind of way. And I immediately did what I'd been trained to do, which was to tell my mum, who told our neighbour, who told her son who was massive and into rugby. And I'm pretty sure he must have thumped that kid, because the sight of me made him noticeably anxious after that. But even though no one bullied me (and I know now how unusual that is), I still felt like I was revealing a shameful secret whenever I had to take off the leg. I still felt intensely vulnerable, every time.

Then, as I got older, another way of being presented itself.

I haven't mentioned crutches, have I?

Crutches are **the best**. If you're missing the whole of one leg, which of these sounds more natural? Either you can strap a fake leg around your bum with Velcro and learn to balance on it, and then, slowly, to lurch. Or you can use the limbs you do have to do the job of the one you don't: you can use crutches to walk with your arms.

When I got home from school, exhausted from dragging my false leg around all day, and more likely than not rubbed raw from the socket, I'd take off my leg and pick up my crutches. And what a relief that was! Crutches may sound like hard work, but if you use them every day your body soon adapts. Your arms and shoulders muscle up until they can easily carry your weight, and the skin on your palms toughens: pretty soon your shoulders stop aching and your hands stop blistering, and then crutches are just how you walk. Or run . . .

By the end of primary school, I was nimble and quick on my sticks, in a way I never could be on my leg. The problem was that I wasn't supposed to use crutches. The doctors and the prosthetists had communicated to my parents that crutches were just a way of avoiding using the leg, and that we amputees **had** to use the leg for our long-term good. Who knows what problems crutches would cause for our bodies as we grew? It was supposed to be obvious that wearing a fake leg – dressed up as a real leg – was the natural, sensible thing to do.

Well, maybe. Although . . . the part of the body that the false leg attaches to isn't **necessarily** longing to be part of a leg again – it feels no urgent desire to be walked on (not in my case, anyway). Sewn-up flesh and severed nerves and bones aren't always thrilled at the prospect of weight-bearing and being pounded into a pulp inside a socket. And though legs may have been designed for walking, arms can adapt to the task pretty well, if they're healthy and whole. But that's not an argument I could have found words for, even if I'd known the truth of it when I was a kid.

So, wearing crutches instead of the leg at school had to be an act of rebellion. No one seemed to think it was a good idea, and I couldn't have just decided to do it unprompted. I would have felt like I was going against the wishes of my parents, and in some odd way, betraying the prosthetists who knew what was best for me . . .

It had to start by accident, then.

I think the first step was at a birthday party on a weekend. Maybe I was ten or eleven. There was a game of football in a sports hall, with a soft, indoor ball. I'd have been on crutches because there were trampolines, too, and trampolining with a through-hip prosthesis was a recipe for pancaking your vertebrae. Anyway, I was on crutches, and I took an experimental swing at the ball. Reader, I toe-poked it straight into the top corner. And as far as I can remember, that was it: my eureka moment.

The next step was seeing a football competition advertised at the school summer fete: '£5 if you can score a penalty kick against a teacher!' I made a plan to go on crutches, without my false leg.

The plan grew in my mind. Each penalty taker would get five kicks. Despite having been virtually unable to kick a football on my leg and having been an awkward bystander at every school football lesson ever, I was fairly sure that on crutches I'd score all of them. That would be £25, thank you very much. I pored over the toys section in the Argos catalogue to see what my winnings would get me.

When the moment came, things did not go as planned. Again, none of the other kids teased me. I think they were curious – maybe even impressed. It's just that they were all watching – of course they were! – and I realised, as soon as I took my first kick, that I'd never tried to kick a real football before.

This real ball was far heavier than the soft, indoor one. The most I could do was to send it rolling gently towards the goal. On my fifth and final kick, which was meandering harmlessly wide of the post, some older kid sitting next to the goal popped the ball into the net and everyone cheered. I remember cringing with embarrassment, but it probably helped us all out of what must have been an awkward situation. At that point, a supportive laugh and a 'well done for having a go' were about the best I could hope for. Perhaps my false leg was grinning to itself, back home on my bedroom floor: 'And you think I have impossible dreams?'

The football had been a humiliation, but still, something had been accomplished. I'd stood up in front of what had felt like the whole school, as myself. No tricks, no secrets, no trying to fit in – just me with my trouser leg hitched up, standing there on my one leg and my crutches. The genie was out of the bottle.

It was another year or two before I finally split with the leg, but I can remember my sense of relief when I did. And I felt no shame. No vulnerability, either. What I felt, was utter, unshakeable confidence. No more dragging my anchor with me. No more climbing the stairs one slow step at a time. No more being left behind to go at my own pace. No more staying in the classroom at break time, because the lurch to the lunch hall felt too far.

Honestly, it felt like flying.

Instead of dreading every journey between classrooms, I relished them. Now I was going to travel with panache. The doors had metal kickplates at the bottom to protect the wood – I kicked them open without breaking stride, so that they slammed back against the walls as I passed. What teacher could protest?! I didn't walk up the stairs, I ran. They go more easily with a little momentum behind you in any case, but to go from one step at a time to two or three . . . Odd for a staircase or a door to be a thing of joy, but for me they were. The sudden joy you feel with freedom.

For a decade after that, I hardly touched the leg.

I started playing football properly on crutches with my friends at weekends. We bought train tickets round Europe after we finished school, and juggled our football through Milan and Venice and Barcelona and Prague. I remember running up the hundreds of steps at Montmartre in Paris without breaking too much of a sweat.

I learned to sing and play the guitar so that I could busk and hitchhike my way round the South of France, at first with a friend and then on my own. Having one leg proved to be a bonus for both of those. To my surprise and relief, it didn't seem to be any kind of disadvantage with girls, either – in fact, it seemed to have the effect of signalling hidden depths of character, whether real or otherwise!

I took a gap year and travelled solo around India. My parents seemed to have warmed to the idea of crutches by this time as they just seemed proud of me, though perhaps it was more relief that I'd come home again (this was just before mobile phones came along, and I only called them every few weeks to let them know I was still alive).

I did take my leg to university, but for one reason only. On Thursdays I would run from my college, on my crutches, right across to the sports centre on the other side of town, where my leg lived in a locker. I'd strap it on for two hours of badminton, then cram it back in the locker and run all the way back to the college bar in time for last pints. And if that's still not super-crippy enough, there's more: I briefly played football for England (international amputee football on crutches – it's a thing). I was always rubbish at penalties, though.

The inspirational spiel isn't the point, though. The point is this: none of it was pre-ordained. I could have stayed on my fake leg. I could have learned to use a free knee and maybe passed as two-legged. I could have walked slowly and evenly through my teens and early twenties looking more-or-less normal. I still wonder how different my life would have been.

Then again, how would my life have been had I worked this all out sooner? I should have been playing football every lunch break from when I started primary school. I'd have played a lot more times for England if I had! But I'm just so relieved that I worked it out when I did. Because once you buy into that idea of hiding your disability and fitting in, it's hard to let go of it. And if you don't let go of it, what might you miss?

Now, I use my leg every day. My robot leg is a tool. It doesn't dream of being a real leg. It has a scuffed old rubbery foot for balance (bare – no shoe), a steel shaft with a fixed knee, and a black socket that always seems to be covered in unicorn stickers. It straps on outside of my clothes, so I can take it off whenever I want, and I wear it to free my hands. I have two small girls to feed and tidy up after, and my wife uses a wheelchair, so my hands are needed.

But I leave the leg at home when I go out. For outside, I have a pair of beautiful black titanium crutches, made just for me.

A Word to Live By for a Young Imani

by Imani Barbarin

United States

Dear Imani,

Mom has always told you about the importance of words. You know what she says: 'Once you speak something into the world, you cannot take it back.' Once you write words down, put pen to paper, those words exist within the world to be made real, travelling from your mind to the page.

Let me guess where you are as you read this. You're eleven years old, so probably seated at the kitchen table stewing over an empty page in a composition notebook. Mom is cooking in the kitchen or, if not, standing directly over you as you finish her assignment. Of course, her giving you extra homework after school irritates you – after all, you've already spent a long day in the classroom and have two or three hours of homework your actual teachers assigned ahead of you. As hard as it is to accept now, she's doing the right thing. (I can tell you she later becomes a teacher in elementary school and finds an outlet for that educational energy, if it's any relief.)

Mom wants you to do a 'free write'. To write about anything you want. The freedom before you is intimidating and your mind starts wandering. Your brother before you, given the same assignment, has chosen protest instead, but you just want to get it over with. Maybe choose the memory of a feeling. Maybe choose one word you have complicated feelings about.

Words can be like magic or a curse, though Mom would never use that term. They have the power to captivate and free, demolish or create, isolate or embrace – and even when you struggle to find them, they are there, waiting for you to come out to play like a friend you've known since kindergarten. You've learned their curves and edges. Words can be warm embraces, daggers, inclusion or a pathway back home. You decide how you want to use them, how to pluck them from your mind to navigate where you are and direct you to where you want to be. They impact your life in real ways: in school, in relationships, and they even turn strangers into friends. Know their power, and handle with care.

Last week, you were on your way home from school, just minding your business, when a man grabbed your arm above the cuff of your crutch and pulled you off to the side. You had heard him praying and preaching, standing on top of a stool he must have brought along for the occasion, and shouting to people as they passed by. You wanted to avoid him so you kept your head down, allowing the words to fly past your ears. But it wasn't until now – now that he had grabbed your arm and pulled you close to him – that you could make out the words he was saying, and that his prayer had turned to you.

You had been walking home with Mom but she was a few steps ahead. It was normal for you to lag behind, and for Mom to listen out for the sound of your crutches as you walked. She would have to notice soon that you were no longer behind her . . .

The man looked at you only briefly before beginning to preach to the people around you. 'And Lord!' he shouted to the heavens, not breaking the rhythm of his preaching. 'Heal this young lady of all her differences! She is special in your eyes and should not have to come to know what the world will impress upon her – these "**disabilities**!"' He spat out the word as though it was dirty and cursed. You were confused as to why he basically said the same thing three times. But you noticed that 'disability' was the only word he seemed to choke out. He could scorn the world as a warning and speak of the ugliness of demons and destruction at the end of time, and still it sounded as though 'disability' was the word that had inspired the most anger. It was confusing, but this preacher was not the first person to say the word disability with disgust. Like a curse to be rid of.

Why is it so bad? You don't feel bad about your disability. Why is it such a horror for others to describe?

For the past week straight, it has been bothering you. It's a thought that keeps nagging at you from the corner of your mind, distracting when you should be practising viola or starting on this evening's homework. But as you sit at the kitchen table with a blank notebook before you, all the thoughts about that man and his hatred of 'disability' are swirling in your head. Now that you have the time and notebook space to write about it, words fail you. Maybe you could just start with the word 'disability'.

The word 'disability' is a universe within five syllables.

You know it means skipping recess occasionally to have physical therapy. It means being called 'special' from time to time, even if no one can explain quite what they mean when they use the word. It often means getting stopped in the street for someone's thoughts about your crutches, or a prayer.

You have heard it your entire life but haven't really thought of the word and all its meanings. It is like the word 'disability' follows you around, labels and becomes you: at the doctor's office, in the meetings you attend with Mom and teachers to discuss disability accommodations and learning plans, and when it comes time to have surgery, or even just to climb the stairs. It means pain and people staring at you. Sometimes it means that your legs won't listen to you. Other times it means you get lonely – and because of the strange things people say to you, sometimes it means you will welcome that loneliness and the peace it can give you.

The way those interactions shape your view of disability is like a playlist on repeat. Sometimes the music gets louder and louder and overwhelms and scares you. That is OK. Those times will pass, and new songs will be added, as others share their own playlists with you. Over time you will come to know other disabled people:

disabled Black people, disabled queer people, disabled women, disabled scientists, disabled people that work at the coffee shop.

Disabled people exist everywhere.

In your time, in 2000, TV shows and movies don't do much to show what life would be like as an adult with a disability. Beyond high school, it all seems to be a big blank spot you'll be walking into. No one explains to disabled kids what will become of people like us. I know Mom and Dad encourage you to have dreams and goals for the future, but you need something more. You need another disabled person to tell you what the possibilities actually are.

Think about what it's like to go to church and see the other disabled Black girl there. It's cool to see someone with a fully lived life with roots and family and autonomy and freedom. She's one of the daughters of the choir soloist. As you grow older, her life develops right in front of you. First, she'll finish school, then she'll come back and start to go to service with her fiancé, and then you'll begin to see her with her daughters. You'll know that even if your life doesn't look exactly like hers in the future, there's at least one version of possibility that feels real, like something to hold on to. It may not become your future. But it is a disabled future that exists before you, giving you permission to dream.

Just like the empty pages at the dinner table that Mom wants you to fill with words, the possibilities intimidate you, but also excite you.

I won't give away too much about your future, but I can say that you will become more comfortable in your own skin, more comfortable with your disability. You will use this confidence to form community and connections with those who are also proud of the term 'disability' and this will shape how you navigate your future.

'Disability' can mean whatever it needs to mean to you. While strangers find a heaviness and burden to the word, it can offer answers and meaning for how you live your life. It doesn't have to be all good, covered in the sugary sweetness of false compliments or accolades. But it also doesn't have to be all bad, a sign of horror and faithlessness. You get to write it.

Sometimes disability just is. Disability just is as you are. It doesn't have to hold meaning outside of the definitions you set for yourself. But it can mean a world of disabled people working together to figure it out.

Disability is a universe, Imani, and you are a part of it.

Smile

by Kendra Winchester

United States

The moment I see the sign for the children's hospital, I slink down in my seat. I hate doctor's appointments.

'Hey, Chickie,' my mom says from the driver's seat. I turn my head to look at her. Mom has that expression she always has when she's trying really hard to not sound annoyed. 'I said, when we get to the doctor's office, I need you to be nice.' She puts a lot of emphasis on 'be' and 'nice'.

I roll my eyes. 'Aren't I always nice?' I say.

Mom clutches the steering wheel harder as she says, 'No, you always try to be a smart alec. Please, don't embarrass me this time.'

'I'll try.'

'No,' she says with a no-nonsense look on her face. 'You'll obey.'

Today is not the day to push. **Sure, whatever,** I think. But I know better than to say it out loud.

As Mom turns into the hospital complex, I see the glass front doors of the lobby entrance and hold my breath. Our minivan spirals down into the underground parking garage, and I drop lower into my seat.

Mom glances over at me again as she looks for a place to park. 'Can you at least try to have a better attitude? Could you at least try to smile?'

Inside I feel anger coiling in my chest. If I try to answer her now, I know I will explode.

My mom pulls into a parking spot. 'If you want to go to camp later this summer, I need you to make an effort.'

I close my eyes tight. I don't want to be in this fancy hospital in the city with its well-dressed staff. I feel frumpy in my second-hand, oversized clothes. I hate standing out. I can't stand the way the doctor looks at me and my mom, like we should be grateful he's even agreed to see hillbillies like us.

But all that stands between me and one glorious week of summer camp is this doctor's appointment. At camp there aren't any doctors or blood tests. The other kids don't make fun of the fact that I'm homeschooled because I'm so sick. No one cares about my clothes. I can just be me.

After my mom parks, I hold my breath and step out of the van.

***

For as long as I can remember, I've had migraines. If you've ever had an ice-cream headache, it's sort of like that. But with migraines, loud noises and bright lights can make your head hurt even more. Some people get sick to their stomach or throw up with their migraines. For me, focusing on things like reading or doing math makes my head feel like my skull is too small for my brain. I feel sure that one day my head is going to suddenly burst from the pressure I feel in my skull.

A few years ago, my mom and I made the two-and-a-half-hour trip from our little home in the Appalachian Mountains, along the Ohio River, into the big city to see my migraine doctor for the first time. When I walked into the Cincinnati Children's Hospital, I marvelled at the colourful artwork and countless windows. I had never seen such a big hospital! And it was all just for kids like me. Looking at all the other sick kids around me made me feel like I was in the right place.

But, I remember, as Mom and I rode up elevators and wandered down a maze of corridors, the bright colourful world of the entryway had turned into a suffocating beige without a window in sight. Walking into my doctor's office, I felt a little disappointed. Where had all the colours gone? How could such a fancy doctor have such a boring waiting room?

Dr Kaufmann is a neurologist – so, basically, a brain doctor. And since he works with kids, he is a paediatric neurologist. He has a reputation for being one of the best migraine specialists in the country.

I've been going to doctors since I was a little kid. Few of them have helped with my migraines, but I was sure that Dr Kaufmann would be different. I thought he would have a magic pill and – **poof!** – my migraines would be gone!

But there was no magic pill or instant cure. Instead, the first time I saw him, Dr Kaufmann ordered test after test. I had to have an MRI, which made me feel like I was in one of the sci-fi movies my dad liked to watch. I had to lie on a table that went into a tube that made really loud noises. But the nurse gave me some large headphones that went completely over my ears. The headphones were attached to a pair of large goggles that went over my eyes. When I put everything on, I realised I could watch cartoons on the inside of the goggles.

Then I had to go to the lab where a nurse stuck me with a needle, and I watched my blood flow into tubes that had stoppers in all the different colours of the rainbow. The nurses always had so many different Band-Aids to choose from, and the nurse let me pick out a cute sticker. As far as tests go, that wasn't so bad.

When we got the test results back, Dr Kaufmann told me it would probably take a long time to find the right combination of medications that would help my migraines.

So, after that first appointment, we tried many different combinations. Now, every day, I stare at all the different coloured pills I have to take and wonder why I am even taking them. None of them seem to help, and every time we try a new medication, and it doesn't work, I feel a little more hopeless.

I know I should just be grateful for the sacrifices my parents make to be able to afford to take me to this very expensive doctor, but I don't see the point in coming all the way to Cincinnati when Dr Kaufmann doesn't seem to be actually helping me. However, I have nowhere else to go.

***

Today, Dr Kaufmann enters the room and sits down on his little rolling stool. One of the wheels squeaks louder than the others as he rolls over towards where I sit on the exam table. Dr Kaufmann greets my mom and asks about the drive. When he turns to me, I look down at my worn jeans and fiddle with the bottom of my faded black T-shirt. I try to hide how anxious I feel sitting in front of this fancy doctor in my rumpled clothes.

Every time I move, the paper on the exam table crinkles and sticks to my skin. I hate that sound. It reminds me of how much of my life I've spent in doctors' offices. They're always wanting to feel my abdomen or peer into my eyes with a bright light. I don't like being touched. I don't like things that are too loud or too bright. It all just makes my migraines worse.

While Dr Kaufmann tests my reflexes and sense of touch, I stare at a picture of Babar the Elephant hanging on the wall behind his shoulder. I take deep breaths and wish Babar could be my doctor. I imagine that he would be the kindest doctor in the world.

'It wouldn't hurt you to smile a little,' Dr Kaufmann says in that tone he uses when he's trying to make a joke. When I don't respond, he takes a deep breath and rolls back. 'So, how's your new medication going?' he asks.

When I don't respond, Dr Kaufmann turns to my mom. She glances at me and says, 'The new meds seem to be fine, right?'

For a moment, we sit in awkward silence. 'I can't remember things,' I blurt out, breaking the tension that has been smothering the room. 'I can't remember things anymore.'

'What?' Dr Kaufmann asks, tilting his head to the side.

'Since you put me on this new medication, I can't remember things. And I can't memorise new things anymore.'

'Well, that happens to a lot of kids in puberty, especially girls,' he says.

'Not like this,' I say. 'This isn't **my** normal. It's awful.' I feel frustrated. Why won't he just believe me? I finally look up and see my mom's face. I know that at least she believes me. Mom will always be on my side.

Dr Kaufmann wheels himself over to the front of the room. He settles in, resting his ankle on his knee. I notice his dress sock slinking down his ankle. He takes a moment before looking at my mom and me.

'So, I am gathering that you feel like you are having some difficulties,' he says. He always has this look on his face after he says something – like he feels that he has just said something really important. I think my mom notices he does this too, because, whenever Dr Kaufmann says something like this, she has a look on her face that she gets when she's trying not to roll her eyes.

I look at Dr Kaufmann, and I imagine how he must see my mom and me: the image we make in our second-hand clothes and Walmart shoes. We are too poor, too rural to be taken seriously. I'm a kid, a girl even. How can I be taken seriously by a famous paediatric neurologist? I feel angry and emotionally spent all at the same time.

I press my mouth into a thin line.

'Well, why don't we wait and see,' my mom says, trying to make peace. 'If she still feels like this next time, we can try something else. Does that sound OK?'

'Yeah, sure,' Dr Kaufmann says dismissively.

'Does that sound OK, Chickie?' Mom says.

I look at my mom and repeat Dr Kaufmann's words, 'Yeah, sure.' I look back at Dr Kaufmann, making eye contact.

I know that next time I still won't be able to remember things. And Dr Kaufmann will still brush it off. But I am done fighting for the day.

***

On our way home from the hospital, we stop to get ice cream. It's become our post-doctor visit tradition.

I gaze into the display case at United Dairy Farmers. All of the different ice cream flavours shimmer behind the glass.

'I would like a scoop of the Blue Moo Cookie Dough and a scoop of the Cotton Candy,' I say to the guy behind the counter. When he hands me a bowl filled with blue ice cream, all of my anxiety melts away, at least for a few minutes.

'Are those flavours bright enough for you?' Mom says, smiling.

'Yeah, I think so,' I say, smiling back.

We climb back into the minivan with our bowls, and I hum with happiness. Is there anything better than a bowl of ice cream on a hot summer day? After a few minutes, I say quietly, 'I really am forgetting things.'

My mom nods as she says, 'I know, Chickie. I know.'

A few weeks later

The moment I step out of the van and into the cool mountain air, it feels like I'm coming home. Every late July, I come back to my favourite sleep-away camp. There's nothing like summers in West Virginia.

After checking in, I head to my cabin to meet up with my friends. As we unpack our suitcases and show off all the snacks we've brought, we catch up about everything that has happened over the last year.

'I **love** choir. Rehearsals are a lot of fun. **And** we get this incredible party at the end of the year,' my friend Amanda says, gesturing wildly. Amanda is expressive and full of joy. I wish I could have half the confidence that she does. 'But tell me about what you've been doing,' Amanda says as she tries to wrangle her sleeping bag onto her bunk.

I pause as I unpack my ridiculous number of mini blue sports drink bottles. My mind flashes back to all of my doctor's appointments, and the big yearly tests I'll have to do again that fall. 'Not much. My brother is still a pain in the butt. But that's about it.'

'Aw, come on,' she says. 'There has to be something.'

'Nope. Just boring Ohio stuff. Not much else.'

'Well, we're about to change that,' she says looking over her handiwork. I wasn't sure if she intended her sleeping bag to look like a rumpled nest or if this was a this-is-as-good-as-it's-gonna-get situation. 'We have a whole week to do whatever we want!'

Everything about camp is wonderful. My friends and I ride horses up and down the mountain trails. When we go white-water rafting, we float down the New River, digging our feet into the sides of the raft as we plunge into the rapids.

But, to me, the best part is the hours of free time that we have every afternoon. We swim in the pond or hang out by the snack bar – and, better yet, I never think about my migraines, at least most of the time.

Every day after breakfast and dinner, I have to pick up my meds from the nurse's office. Her office is in the corner of the gym, right near the basketball court. Everyone can see the kids lining up to get their meds. I hate it when other kids see me in line and ask me, 'What's wrong with you?' So, this year, I know that if I am going to avoid prying questions, I have to get to the nurse's office before everyone else finishes eating.

For most of the week, I manage to get to the nurse's office early, before everyone else. I feel proud of myself for avoiding any prying looks or invasive questions from the other kids. But, one morning, everything goes wrong.

That day, my cabin arrives late for breakfast. We're one of the last cabins to start eating. I worry over my soggy tater tots as I look around the room and realise that we are the last campers left in the cafeteria.

When I finally open the gym door after breakfast, the room's humidity hits me like a wave, and the sound of basketballs and screaming kids hurts my ears. I'm too late. Somehow, the line at the nurse's office has grown longer than I've ever seen before. As I reluctantly join the other kids waiting for their medication, I keep my eyes on the polished gym floor and hope no one will see me.

When I look up, I see the nurse's office with its door open. Rows of brown paper bags line the shelves on one side of the office. The nurse sits in a chair near the front door, helping campers find their bags. But I have so many medications, my mom had put all of my prescription and vitamin bottles in a clear plastic bag. I always feel embarrassed to ask the nurse for it.

When there are only three or four kids ahead of me, I'm

close enough to the nurse's office to hear her and the male counsellor in the room. He picks up my clear gallon bag and peers in at my vitamin and prescription bottles. 'Wow, look at this one!' he says to the nurse. 'There are so many.'

The nurse glances over to see what he's holding. 'Yeah,' she says as she helps a camper sign for his medication.

'Do you think they actually need all of these?' asks the counsellor.

'No, probably not,' the nurse replies as she helps the camper stuff his sign-in sheet back into his paper bag.

As I listen to the conversation, a roaring fills my ears. I can't believe what I'm hearing. I look at the other campers around me who must have heard the counsellor, too. I feel a tight spring in my chest, my anger coiling inside me. Soon it's my turn to get my medications.

'Name?' asks the nurse.

As I struggle to keep my anger in check, I tell her my name and say loudly in the direction of the counsellor, 'That's mine. The big clear one right there.'

The counsellor's eyes bug out of his head. His face goes

pink. **Good**. I think. **You should be embarrassed**.

'Do you need help getting them out of the bottles?'
asks the nurse as she glances in the direction of the
counsellor.

'No,' I say as I walk over to the counter in the office,
pulling out the different bottles. I turn my head towards
the counsellor. 'And, yes, I do need them,' I say coldly.

'Oh, yeah, sure,' the counsellor mumbles.

After I finish counting out all of the pills, I hold them
in my left hand and sign the form with my right. I give
the counsellor one last look before I head to the water
fountain and swallow all my pills at once.

As I walk away from the nurse's office to the stage on
one side of the gym, I clench my jaw and glare at the
shiny hardwood floor. Camp is supposed to be my safe
space, but that counsellor and the nurse have just
ruined it.

I sit down on the edge of the stage with my friends.
My thoughts swirl around, creating angry knots in my
chest. Amanda looks over at me. 'Hey, what's wrong?'
she asks.

'What do you mean?' I say.

'You just don't look happy,' she says.

So, I explain. And, as I tell Amanda what happened at the nurse's office, she looks horrified.

'That's awful! I would be so mad too!'

'You would?' I ask.

Amanda nods her head vigorously. 'Oh, yeah, so mad. And I can't believe a counsellor said that. Do you want to go talk to someone about it? Like our counsellor or the program director?'

I shrug and shake my head at the same time. 'Nah, I just want to forget about it. But thanks anyway.'

'Okay, whatever you want. And if you change your mind, I'll go with you.'

The tight coil in my chest begins to ease. Amanda smiles at me and nudges me with her shoulder. 'It's OK, pal. You don't have to do this alone.'

Camp might not be the safe place I have always imagined in my head. And there will always be doctors or nurses who don't believe me when I tell them how I'm feeling or what I need. But there are also people like Amanda and my mom. And I know they are always going to be there for me.

I watch the other kids playing basketball and chatting together on the bleachers. Then I turn, look at my friends, and smile.

How to Belong

by Alex Wegman

United States

When you think of an athlete, what do you picture? Fitness, agility, speed, strength and co-ordination come to mind, right? Composure? Confidence? Fast reflexes? Well, this is a story about a girl who possessed almost none of those.

It's me. I'm the girl. And I was born into a family of athletes.

I've used a wheelchair since I got too big for a stroller. My parents noticed my development wasn't moving along like it should when I was a little under a year old and not rolling over or reaching for my toes, the way babies who are going to walk usually do. They took me for some tests and were told by doctors that I was a disabled baby, and would be disabled for the rest of my life. When my mom and dad got that news, they didn't let go of their expectations that I'd be a busy, happy kid with friends and my own interests, so I had a pretty typical childhood when it came to those things. One of the ways they helped to foster that was by sharing their interests with me.

***

I grew up in Minnesota, USA, a state with a reputation for gritty, active, outdoorsy citizens. Dad was a gym rat. My brother played hockey and football (the American kind) and my sister played hockey and volleyball. And my mom? She ran cross-country and track, high jumped, biked, rollerbladed, skied and snowshoed. She also played broomball, which is kind of a cross between ice and field hockey: you wear sneakers with suction cups on the soles, and you hit a ball around an ice rink with a broom. (Yes, it's weird, but when you live in a state that transforms into a frozen tundra for half the year, you'll turn just about anything involving ice and a stick into a sport.) Oh, and she played softball, too (less weird, and requires no explanation). Actually, she still does most of those things.

Mom's an upper limb amputee, born with no right arm from just above her elbow, and sports were obviously, naturally her thing. So from disabled mom to disabled kid, I was always being encouraged to try new sports at the local adaptive recreation centre, which was called Courage Center at the time. It was a magical, fully accessible building forty minutes from my house, with a pool, gymnasiums, physical, occupational and recreational therapy, camps, driving instructors, a lending closet for things like track wheelchairs and handcycles and more. I wanted to be like my mom, and Courage Center was the very best place to try.

First, I tried swimming. It seemed like it should be a natural fit – we had a pool in the backyard and my grandparents lived on a lake. But it didn't last long because the second I couldn't touch the pool bottom and wasn't wearing a life jacket, my mom saw my life flash before her eyes and made an executive decision to call it quits. I love the water and I'm a decent swimmer now, but it wasn't going to be my childhood claim to athletic fame.

Then, adaptive karate. I liked wearing a gi and memorising forms, which are kind of like martial arts dance routines. I advanced to an orange belt with a stripe, but I couldn't handle my chair well enough to participate in higher levels while seated, and I wasn't steady enough on my feet to spar, so there wasn't much further I could go. I also talk a lot. Like, so much. That's often frowned upon in martial arts environments.

At our annual adaptive sports day camp, I tried

wheelchair softball, wheelchair tennis, wheelchair racing, wheelchair soccer (football), adaptive rock climbing, riding a three-wheeled bike, sled hockey, shot put, javelin, waterskiing, kayaking, canoeing – if you can name it, I've probably given it a shot. I discovered that most wheelchair sports are really challenging if your upper body is disabled in the ways mine is.

As my Courage Center pals found and mastered their sports and my mom continued to succeed at every athletic endeavour she attempted, I absolutely floundered. A season of this, a few practices of that – aside from my three years of martial arts, nothing stuck.

Mom and I are a funny pair; both physically disabled, totally by chance, in very different capacities. Her athleticism outshines mine in ways that I've always thought probably go far beyond disability, but it's hard to know, isn't it? I mean, she consistently beats me at things like croquet and beanbag toss, games at which we should be pretty evenly matched, disabled or not.

It's good we were always able to talk about it, because the difference between our disabilities could have made all this pretty tricky. Mom had grown up with a 'there's no such thing as can't' philosophy, but she'd left it behind by the time she became a parent and totally respected that my limitations were wildly different from hers. That's not to say she was all 'everyone gets a trophy', either: she understood the importance of hard work, and expected me to apply myself and do my very best, however that looked. Phoning it in wasn't an option. She wanted me to feel the same sense of accomplishment and belonging in sports that she did, I think, and worked really hard to make sure I stood a chance of finding my place. Then, when I was nine, I did. I went to my first wheelchair basketball practice, and I played for the next seven years.

I am not physically cut out to be a basketball player in any way. I have poor control of my fingers, my upper body is weak, and my lower body is weak **and** spastic. I'm partially paralysed basically everywhere below my neck. An incomplete quadriplegic. Quad, for short. Not a good candidate to pass and catch a ball at long distances, race up and down the court against kids with more arm strength, and throw a ball into a hoop ten feet in the air.

So why in the world did I stick with it for so long?! Basketball was a lot of things, both positive and negative. It kept my hands tough and calloused, which is a huge advantage if you push a wheelchair all the time.

It gave me a way to, for the first time, really use my body for active play. It taught me about my wheelchair and sports equipment – saving and fundraising, care, and maintenance. It was exercise and fitness training. But it also brought me a lot of insecurity around the way my quad body moves and how limited its capacity to build strength and co-ordination is. At my school, I was by far the most able-bodied wheelchair user. At basketball, I was by far the least.

Mostly, though, basketball was community. I had found my people. I had found the only space where I knew I wouldn't be the only person like me. My friends from basketball knew all about being the only disabled kid in homeroom. They knew how embarrassing it felt to have their bladders fail on a school field trip; how annoying it was to always be seated close to a door, at the end of a row; how awful it was to sit through meetings while a bunch of adults talked about the limited ways they'd be 'included' in gym class, school dances and emergency planning. They knew, as well as I did, that for all the praise they received about being inspiring or resilient, they really just wanted to be kids who were automatically part of things, the way their non-disabled friends were.

Wheelchair sports flipped what felt like an unchangeable script. We all knew how to dismantle each other's wheelchairs – a favourite pastime was yanking a wheel off an unsuspecting teammate's chair and cackling as they crashed to the ground while onlookers gasped. No one and nowhere was safe. Hotel lobby? Bye-bye, wheel. Restaurant parking lot? You might be rolling along without a care in the world and then all of a sudden be on your back on the concrete because someone grabbed you from behind and tipped you over. It reminded us we were in an exclusive club, and we loved it. And when our non-disabled friends came to practices and tournaments to cheer us on, they were the ones who had to work to find ways to be included. 'Gimp' was our favourite slang word, reclaiming an ableist insult that had long been used against disabled people. We were proud to be gimps, and that word, which rightfully made other people cringe (and which they knew they could never use), became our official seal.

It wasn't all teasing and harassment, either, as fun as that was. My teammates had access needs very much like mine, which meant their homes were useable by me! We had a network of homes we could all enter, mostly without assistance. When an invitation for a birthday party or a sleepover came from one of us, nobody had to worry about getting left out or left behind. 'I'd invite you to my party, but . . .' became unacceptable, because we proved to each other it didn't have to be that way. Basketball was the world that brought most of us our first by-default inclusion, and it raised the bar for my social life.

We came from all over the state to practise on Saturday mornings, and afterwards we often went to see a movie. There was a movie theatre that gave free admission to wheelchair users because of some sort of legal settlement related to the Americans with Disabilities Act (the disability access law in the United States). Naturally, we nicknamed it 'The Gimp Theatre'. One by one, we'd roll up to the box office window, still dirty and sweaty from practice, and ask for a ticket to something our parents would undoubtedly be horrified we'd seen. For whatever reason, the staff had no problem handing fourteen tickets to a film rated R ('Restricted' to seventeen and over) to a bunch of disabled kids aged eleven to sixteen or so. Then on to the auditorium we'd go, a swarm of kids on wheels with no adult supervision – baffling to onlookers, I'm sure.

The first time I held hands with Brendan was in that theatre after practice when I was fourteen. I have no idea what we were seeing, but it didn't matter. He was the only teammate in my year at school, and I was obsessed with his natural orange hair and freckles. His absolutely giant, tough hands could palm a basketball – and my heart. He was so at home on the court. While I was playing on the prep team and struggling to just barely keep up, he was routinely the tournament MVP on the varsity team. But he still liked me! Our brief teen romance ended shortly after he told me he loved me at the end of a phone call and I replied, 'Thank you,' in a panic and hung up. Not very many weeks later, another teammate, Ian, told me he was sorry things with Brendan had ended . . . but . . . that he could be a better boyfriend than Brendan, anyway. And thus began my second wheelchair basketball romance, holding hands in The Gimp Theatre once again.

I got to travel all over the midwestern United States with that weird, chosen, disabled family. Those tournament trips, squeezing our uncooperative bodies into fifteen-passenger vans or zooming around airport terminals with two wheelchairs per kid (one for everyday, one for the court), were a highlight of my childhood. Being one of only two or three girls between the teams (prep, junior-varsity and varsity) was pretty fun, too. I'd never been into dresses, nail polish or make-up, and felt at home with the boys. Plus, they were cute. The travel and downtimes were always the main event for me – rare and precious opportunities to play, rest and flirt with kids I didn't have to explain my body or needs to. We danced at banquets, played endless pranks on each other and our coaches, took risks, got hurt and were regular kids in ways we couldn't imagine outside our sport. Our little calves, puffy ankles and purple feet fitted right in with the bodies of peers we admired and wanted to be like. We saw ourselves – our bodies, our experiences and our futures – represented in each other, in ways we never could with school and church friends.

Like I said earlier, I am not cut out to be a basketball player, and I never was. I'm an adult with my own kids now, and in the years since I stopped playing, I've found many ways better suited for me to be active, such as adaptive mountain biking, camping, surfing and kayaking. I wouldn't trade my years as a worse-than-average basketball player for any of these, though. I'm a proud, confident disabled adult because basketball taught me how to belong and how to demand belonging, something the rest of the world couldn't give me. Except Mom. She knew.

Lobster Girl

by Jen Campbell

United Kingdom

School trips always make me nervous. Mostly, I like
being at school. I like the rules, the timetables and the
smell of textbooks. I know what to expect; I know what
I'm supposed to do. All of those things make me feel
safe.

School trips are different. During school trips, bits of
the outside world creep into the school world and I don't
know how to feel about that. We live in a small village,
so everyone knows each other, and most of the children
in my class live on the same cul-de-sacs. They play in the
streets in the evenings, have water fights over fences in
the summer. I've been invited to join in a couple of times,
but each time I've found it overwhelming. I can't get over
how much everyone shoves each other, racing down
the road and tripping over shoelaces, the cuts and the
bruises, and sometimes worse, all while laughing and
joking and having fun.

'Aren't you worried about breaking something?' I want

to ask. 'Aren't you worried about ending up in the hospital?'

I try not to say these things out loud because I know they will laugh at me. I know that lots of them already think I'm boring. They think I'm a scaredy-cat and a teacher's pet and generally just a bit weird. I try not to mind, and it's easier not to mind when I'm at school. When I'm dressed the same as everyone else, and we're all doing the same things. But school trips aren't like that. Everyone breaks away into their friendship groups from outside school; there's a lot of whispering and joking around, and I feel a bit lost.

I don't mind it as much when we go on trips to learn things, like when we go to Beamish. Beamish is a living museum; it's a huge Victorian town frozen in time. You can walk down its cobbled streets, get on a tram or hop on a steam train. You can go into all its old shops where everyone is an actor dressed up in Victorian clothes. My favourite place in Beamish is the sweet shop, its wooden shelves stacked high with glass jars full of sherbet, humbugs and pear drops, and in the back room they make honeycomb from scratch which smells warm and delicious. If you want to buy something, you put your money in a wooden ball that's lifted onto a pulley, and that ball whizzes around the top of the shelves and out of sight. It's delivered to a hidden shopkeeper, who takes your money out, puts your change in, and sends the wooden ball zooming back down to you. I think it's magic.

There's also a school at Beamish. Whenever we go on a class visit, we go to the school for a pretend lesson, and the Victorian teacher glares at us angrily, threatening to hit us with a ruler if we don't write neatly. She's just acting, of course, but it's very convincing. Last time we were there, she explained how everyone who was left-handed would have been forced to write with their right hand in Victorian times, so the ink didn't smudge.

'And everyone would have been made to hold their pens very precisely, like this,' she held up a pen, pinched delicately between her fingers. 'Let me see you do that.'

Everyone mimicked the way she was holding her pen.

'No, no, not like that,' she tutted, coming over to my desk to correct me. 'You need to hold it like—oh.' She stopped, confused, looking down at my hands.

I knew I shouldn't be embarrassed but my cheeks flushed red. 'I can't hold my pen like that,' I said.

'I see.' She hurried back to the front of the class. I got the feeling she was trying to get away from me as quickly as possible.

'Miss!' someone shouted from the back of the room. 'Miss, if left-handed people were forced to write with their right hand, what would people like Jenny be made to do?'

A couple of people giggled. My body felt like it had pins and needles – it always does that when I feel anxious.

'Well,' the pretend Victorian teacher paused. 'That's why we should be thankful for the wonders of modern medicine, isn't it?' She smiled awkwardly. 'It was a very different world over a hundred years ago. Who knows what would have happened to people like Jenny. Anyway, let's move on to arithmetic . . .'

Gradually, everyone stopped staring at me.

Later that day, before we got the coach home, we visited the fairground, which had a beautiful carousel and a red and white helter-skelter. A couple of children from another class came up to me and pointed at a poster pinned to the Hall of Mirrors. It was for a Victorian 'freak show'. The poster had black and white illustrations of people with disabilities and limb differences, just like me. Some of them were dressed up as animals.

'Shouldn't you be in one of those shows?' one of the children said, and they all fell about laughing.

I don't remember if I said anything in reply. I don't think I did. All I remember is how loud my heart was beating. It was beating so loud it made the rest of the world sound like it was underwater.

***

I was born with a disability called Ectrodactyly-Ectodermal Dysplasia-Clefting syndrome. It affects different parts of my body: my skin, my eyes, my hair, my teeth, my kidneys, and lots of other things, too. But the main thing that people notice is my hands. I was born with the bones and skin of my fingers fused together, and doctors had to create hands for me using metal pins and skin grafts. I have fewer fingers than most people, and the ones I do have are different shapes. I've had over twenty operations, and I spend a lot of time in and out of hospital for scans and physiotherapy.

Although EEC syndrome is a big part of my life, I don't tend to talk about it at school, even with my friends. I don't talk about hospitals, even though sometimes I have to miss school to go to appointments. I don't talk about the hand splints I wear at night, or the eye compresses I do in the morning. I don't talk about the teeth embedded in my jaw, or how my kidneys don't work the same way as other people's. Whenever I try to talk about it, my voice gets stuck. Too many things have happened; the words feel too big. I don't know how to separate everything and put it in some sort of order. I don't know how to explain things in a way that would make sense, in a way that would help people understand. If I try, I can feel the gap between my life and my friends' lives growing bigger and bigger, and that scares me. So, I end up not talking about it at all. As for strangers, I realised a long time ago that most people become uncomfortable if they notice my hands, so usually I smile or tell a joke to try to make them feel better. But that doesn't make me feel better; it makes me want to curl up and hide.

Last year, when we went away for the weekend on a class field trip, my disability accidentally made me a hero. We all got on a bus which took us up into the hills, and we stayed in a rundown building that looked haunted. During the day, we learned how to read maps and we walked around muddy fields wearing itchy socks and borrowed hiking boots. At night, we slept in bunk beds on the third floor of this possibly haunted building, and we were told that if we needed to use the bathroom we'd have to put on our clothes, grab a torch, head down three flights of stairs, go outside and walk across the courtyard to use the outdoor toilet. It was February and it was freezing. Everyone complained. The adults refused to back down.

'Think of it as an adventure!' they said.

We shivered in our pyjamas, remembering the outdoor toilets at Beamish. It certainly felt very Victorian.

Just before we went to sleep, my teacher called me out into the corridor. He made sure the door shut behind me, then he bent down and whispered: 'Jenny, because you've got problems with your kidneys, we don't want you going outside in the cold at night; it's not safe. So, let me show you a secret,' he beckoned for me to follow him around the corner, where – lo and behold – there was a secret corridor with a secret bathroom. It was indoors. It was warm. It even had a fluffy pink toilet seat cover. 'This is just for the teachers,' he said. 'But you can use it, too. Just don't tell anyone else about it, OK?'

I blinked at him. I couldn't believe that these adults were making ten-year-olds trek to an outdoor bathroom, in the winter, when this bathroom was right there. Sometimes, grown-ups are really confusing. So, of course, I promised I wouldn't tell anyone, then I went back into the bedroom and told the rest of the class immediately. Well, I didn't announce it (I'm far too shy for that), but I certainly told a few people, and I told them to spread the word. I got lots of whispered thank-yous and silent thumbs up. Throughout the night, I heard my classmates tiptoeing to the secret bathroom, shushing each other so the teachers didn't hear. I grinned sleepily. Personally, I think everyone deserves not to freeze their knickers off, disability or not.

***

Today, for this year's school trip, we're going to an indoor water park. This isn't one of our educational trips, so I'm not going to be able to hide behind a notebook, but I'm not as nervous as usual because I really like swimming. I've been swimming since I was tiny, and I like how the world goes silent when you push yourself below the surface. The only thing I don't like is diving. I can never trust my body to curve into the water so, whenever I try it, I end up doing a clumsy jump. If I don't pinch my nose in time, the pool water shoots up my nostrils, and I'm violently reminded of operations and gas masks filled with anaesthetic, which makes my body jolt. Did you know that swimming pool water smells like anaesthetic? It's because of all the chlorine. Anyway, that's my least favourite part, but I enjoy the rest. Sometimes I wonder if I like swimming so much because I was born with all my fingers joined together, like a web-toed creature.

We're on our way. Our bus snakes through a tunnel under the river towards the water park, and we pull up beside a huge building with green slides looping in and out of its walls. The slides make the building look like a futuristic machine, and everyone presses their face to the windows to get a better look. Some of the slides look fun, but a lot of them look scary, with loads of twists and big drops. One of them is the fastest water slide in the whole country and, at the back of the bus, a boy in next door's class is saying:

'That slide there is a seventy-degree drop!' His voice is filled with awe. 'And you go down it at thirty miles an hour. How cool is that?'

'That sounds like the beginning of a mathematical equation, Steven!' our teacher calls from the front of the bus. Nearly everyone groans. Our teacher laughs. 'Don't worry, no maths today. Now, go and have fun!'

As soon as we get into our swimming costumes, my friends say they want to go on the big slides near the top of the building. I follow them up several flights of stairs but when I see the slides they're pointing at, I know immediately that I don't want to go on them. The one they're most excited about is called the Hurricane. It's an enclosed tube slide that's so narrow you have to ride it lying down with your arms across your chest. The lifeguard tells everyone not to sit up during the ride because, if you do, you'll bang your head. My friends queue up eagerly, but the round opening of the Hurricane reminds me of scanners at the hospital – climbing into them, being strapped in and lying down in the dark with machines beeping all around me. My heart begins to beat faster. I've got pins and needles in my hands and my feet. The smell of chlorine starts to trick my brain into thinking that something bad is going to happen. I don't want to be there.

'I'm going to go downstairs,' I tell my friends. 'I'm going to go for a swim.'

'But we're not here to swim,' they say. 'We're here to have fun!'

I don't know how to explain that, for me, this isn't fun. 'It's fine,' I say, smiling. 'You have fun; I'll see you later.'

It's easier to breathe when I get back downstairs. This is where the pools are, including a stretch of water called the Lazy River, which loops around the whole building – it even has a small current which gently pushes you along. I pull on my swimming goggles and slip into the warm water. I swim for half an hour and, even though it's quite loud in the water park, somehow, it's like the rest of the world isn't there, and it's very peaceful.

After that, I decide I'll try some of the smaller slides. The park is open as usual, so as well as our school there are also parents with younger children. I feel self-conscious when some of the children I pass ask their mums why I have scars on my legs (from skin grafts), and why I'm wearing swimming goggles when no one else is (because I was born without tear ducts). Even though they're not asking me those questions, I feel a strong urge to turn around and explain myself. Instead, I say nothing and pretend I haven't heard, even as one parent gasps at my hands and pulls her child away from me, as though I'm contagious.

Suddenly, I remember those freak show posters at Beamish last year. I know there were people with my disability in those shows. Audiences used to call them the Lobster Children. My heart starts beating faster again, so I turn around and go back to swimming.

When the teacher calls us up for lunch, I find my friends and we eat French fries, which for some reason taste like the best fries I've ever eaten. I must be hungry from swimming so much. I tell them that the Lazy River is super relaxing, and they grin, telling me about their favourite ride, the Black Hole, which they'd raced down in complete darkness.

'It's like you're whizzing through space!' they giggle. 'It's nuts!'

Afterwards, they say they're all going to go on the Death Drop. That's not the real name of the ride, it's just what everyone calls it. It's the one Steven was talking about on the bus; the fastest water ride in the UK, which looks almost like a sheer vertical drop. That slide is on the top floor of the park, so I walk up the stairs behind my friends, but find myself stopping on the second highest floor where there's a different ride called the Twister. There's a long queue for this one, and I accidentally join the back of it as I move through the crowd. It's the second-fastest slide in the park, but the opening of this slide is a bit bigger than the others, so it doesn't look quite so claustrophobic. I think to myself, **maybe I could**

manage this one? Perhaps I could? I don't know. I feel all tingly. I can't decide what to do.

In the end, I don't make a conscious decision to go for it, I just don't choose to leave the queue. As I get closer to the front, I realise this is a ride you're supposed to do in pairs. I'm on my own. I look around anxiously. The Twister consists of two tunnel slides that wrap around each other, like a hair braid: one person gets in the left-hand slide, one person gets in the ride-hand slide, you both whizz down separately and emerge at the end together. It's not as steep as the Death Drop, but it's still very, very fast.

'Are you two going on together?' The lifeguard nods at me and a person to my right, a girl in my class who I am not friends with – the girl who asked the teacher at Beamish what Victorians would have 'done' with 'someone like me'.

'Erm . . .' I blush.

'Sure, let's go,' the girl pushes her wet hair out of her face and moves towards the right-hand slide like she's done this a thousand times before. Perhaps she has. Trying to suppress my nerves, I go towards the left-hand slide. I can hear the water inside it rushing away into nothing.

'OK,' the lifeguard presses a button, and a countdown begins above each of our slides. 'Hold on to the top of your slide here, so you don't slip down it. When the buzzer goes, let go, and you'll go whooshing down. You're going to go fast, so lie down all the way, do not sit up, and do not breathe in any of the water.' He recites all of this very quickly, as I climb into my slide, holding the top of it to stop myself falling, watching the numbers flash above me: '10, 9, 8, 7 . . .' I can hear my brain starting to panic, trying to talk to the rest of me, trying to ask my body what it's doing – why it has decided to go on this ride. The answer is: I don't really know, but here I am. I am doing it.

'Three, two, one, go!'

A buzzer goes. I let go of the top of the slide and cross my arms on top of my chest. At the last moment, remembering what it's like to dive, I pinch my nose quickly, so the water doesn't go up it. I slip downwards. The ride happens in a rush and a roar. I careen from one side of the tunnel to the other, unsure which way I'm facing, whether I should close my eyes or keep them open. It is terrifying but also exhilarating. The whole thing takes less than ten seconds. I come hurtling out of the slide and glide across a pool of water, gasping. Next to me, the girl from the right-hand slide emerges, too, with a shriek.

'That was insane!' she laughs, pulling herself up.

My legs are like jelly. I clamber out and look down at myself, trying to work out how I feel in this moment. I feel a bit shaky, and I don't want to go on the ride again, but I also feel warm, like there's static running up and down my body.

***

'Hey!' My friends find me later in the changing room. 'We lost you! Did you swim some more?'

'Yeah,' I'm packing my bag and trying to sound casual. 'And I went on the Twister, too.'

'No way!' One of them grabs my arm. 'That one made me feel so dizzy.'

I nod. 'It really throws you around, doesn't it?'

'Yeah, it's wild!'

Someone clears their throat behind us, and we turn to see who it is. It's the girl I went on the Twister with. She's smirking as she does up her school shirt. 'She's totally lying,' she says coolly. 'I saw her in the queue for the

Twister, but when she got to the front, she got scared and ran away.'

My breath catches in my throat. At first, I'm sure she's made a mistake.

'I didn't do that,' I say, confused. 'You and me both went on the Twister together, remember? Are you thinking of someone else?'

She snorts nastily. 'How exactly could I be thinking of someone else? You don't look like anyone else.'

I feel like she's punched me.

My heart feels like it's beating inside of my skull.

Of course she remembers; she's just making fun of me.

Of course she remembers; she just doesn't want people to know that she went on a ride with me.

Me, the Lobster Girl.

My friends look at the girl and then back at me, unsure of what's going on. I open my mouth to say something, but I know that if I speak, I'll probably cry – and that will make her laugh, which will make this all much, much worse.

So, instead, I say nothing – and, looking victorious, she leaves.

My friend puts a hand on my shoulder. 'It doesn't matter if you were too scared to go on that ride, you know.'

I feel a small stab of anger. 'I went on it,' I say quietly. 'I really did.'

'OK,' she shrugs, though I'm not sure she believes me. She pulls a packet of sweets from her rucksack. 'Want one?'

'Sure,' I hold out my hand and she passes me a cola bottle. It fizzes against the roof of my mouth as we walk out of the water park. I focus on the fizzing to distract myself from the pins and needles that have crept back into my body. I glance back at the water slides snaking in and out of the building. The Twister is right near the top, and I stare up at it. Weirdly, it doesn't look as steep or as scary when I look at it from down here.

On the bus ride back to school, I think about all the things I could have said, both to my friends and to the girl. My brain goes over it, again and again, even though I'd rather it didn't. I try to tell myself that it doesn't matter – I know I went on that ride, so who cares, really? Plus, even if I don't forget about this, they will have forgotten about it by tomorrow.

Mostly, though, I wish I'd been able to say to them

that, actually, I've done plenty of scary things in my life. Things that have terrified me much, much more than a water slide. Operations and medical procedures and other things that they couldn't possibly understand. And even though I don't have the words to explain that to them, I am proud of myself for doing those scary things. I am proud of this body of mine.

As the bus goes through the tunnel under the river, I take a deep breath and put my hands in my lap. I try to remember what it was like to swim in the Lazy River earlier that morning. How quiet it was when I dipped my head below the surface. How powerful I'd felt, propelling myself along.

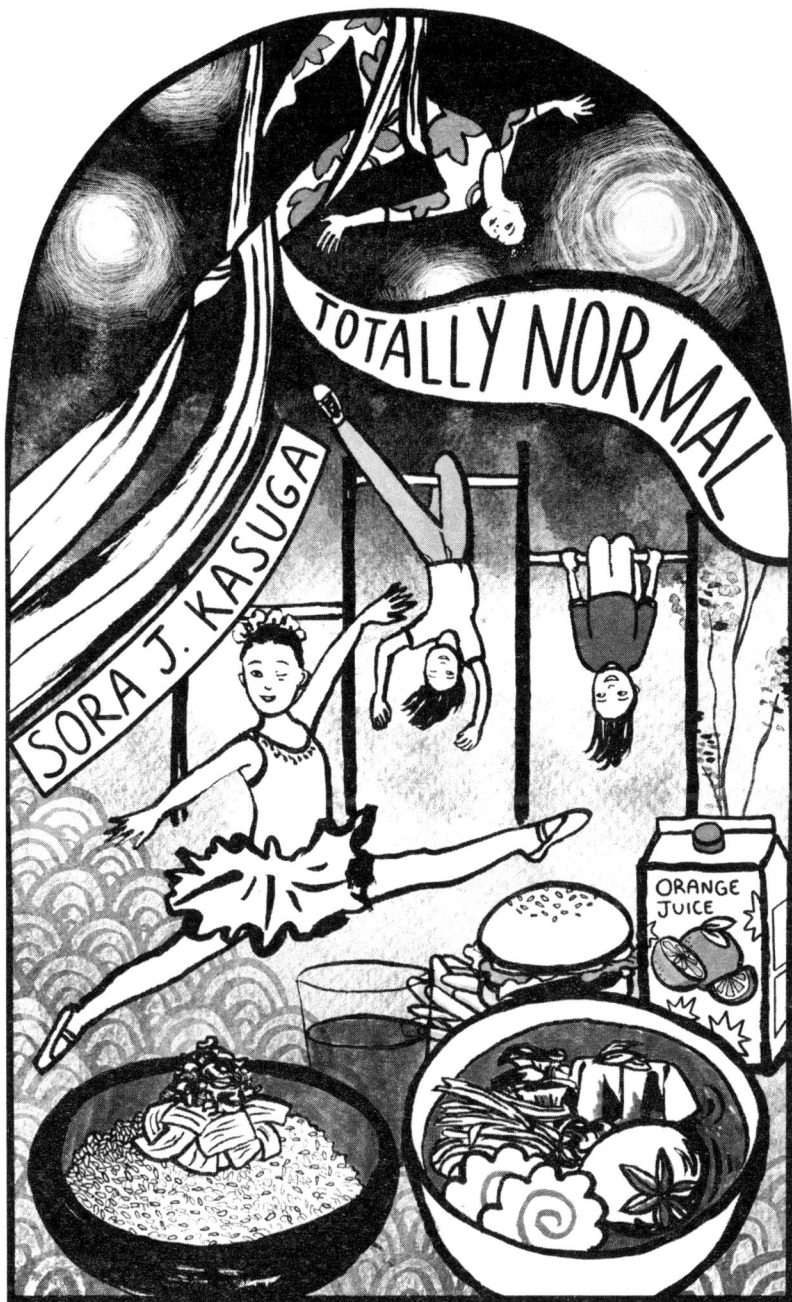

Totally Normal

by Sora J. Kasuga

United States

'**PSSSST!** What's our plan?!'

I felt a sharp elbow in my side. My friend, Daniela, was yelling in a whisper as our class walked through the quiet hallways of our school towards the yard. It was break time! Daniela eyed our teacher warily, her long, dark hair falling across her face.

'Want to go climb around?' I whispered back.

'Yeah!' She grinned.

As soon as we reached the end of the hallway, we burst through the doors into the blazing Arizona sun. We ran as fast as we could for the pull-up bars. It was important to be the first ones there to make our claim. The silver bars stood tall against the blue sky. They were supported by poles that had been red, white and blue at one point. Now, the paint had mostly flaked off. We hung by our knees and our elbows. Sometimes we would hold on with both hands, swinging back and forth before launching ourselves into the soft brown sand beneath us. I loved climbing around. I would pretend to be an Olympic gymnast.

We had just started to figure out how to do multiple flips around the structure when Daniela started looking tired.

'Let's get water!' she said.

'Go ahead,' I said, 'I'll be here when you get back.'

'OK!' She dashed off.

As I dangled under the bar getting ready to try another round of acrobatics, one of the popular kids ran towards me. She had perfect blonde curls and bright blue eyes. She was outgoing. Other girls wanted to be her. I wanted to be her. She never talked to me, so I was surprised to see her come over. She skidded to a halt.

'Let me see your tongue!' she shouted.

I looked around. Daniela was across the yard at the water fountain. Under the bright sun, the bar suddenly became too hot to hold. I let go and dropped down to my feet. Even the sand felt too hot to stand on. How did this girl know my tongue was different? Were other kids talking about me?

I was never good at saying 'no'. It felt rude. But I didn't want to give in, either. What did it matter what my tongue looked like? I paused. I was doomed. If I didn't show her, she could get her whole group to turn against me . . . maybe even the whole school!

Then I thought, **Maybe it wouldn't be so bad if I let her look?** I mean . . . maybe if she knew a little more about me, then maybe we could be friends, right? Maybe if I didn't try to hide anything about myself, she would admire me for my confidence! Maaayyybe she would even tell the rest of the school that everyone should like me!

OK, yeah! I thought, **I'm going to show her I have nothing to hide!** I made myself tall, opened my mouth and let my tongue flop out.

'EEEEWWW!!!' she screamed. She turned around and ran back to her friends, kicking up a cloud of dust that flew into my face. My cheeks were now as hot as the sand and my eyes were watering. Just then, our teacher blew the whistle. Everyone ran to him, lining back up. I was relieved my friend hadn't seen what happened. I didn't want her to worry.

I knew why things like this happened. There were a lot

of 'weird' things about me. I mean, they were weird to **other** people. For me, I was just **me**. I was born with some rare conditions that had no known cause and no known cure. My left cheek was always swollen, like I had just been to the dentist for a cavity. My eyelid was swollen, too. I could barely open it. And I had these things that looked like small, red, rubbery rocks which grew on my eyeball and tongue. Sometimes my eyelid or cheek would turn dark purple.

Those weren't the only 'weird' things, though. My family and I were some of the only Japanese Americans living in our small, military town in Arizona. We did everything we could to act 'American'. None of us spoke Japanese, only English. When friends came over, Mom would cook cheeseburgers and chocolate chip cookies. We only ate Japanese food when no one else was around. I didn't know why, but the people who had blonde hair and blue eyes were the most popular and most successful in my school. I wanted nothing more than to be one of them.

Given all the effort my family and I went through to fit in, it was always confusing when people still didn't think I was American. My family had been here so long! My parents were born here. My grandparents were even born here! It was my great-grandparents that had immigrated to the US. During the Second World War, the US government had locked Japanese Americans in camps because they thought we were the enemy. This included my family. In those camps, my family were taught to be ashamed of our culture, ashamed of ourselves. At home, I felt like I could be proud of my Japanese heritage. Out in public, though, I found myself and my family trying to hide the 'Japanese' part. Likewise, I also tried to hide the fact that I had a facial difference. I wanted to blend in, even though other people made that feel impossible. I didn't talk about these things very often. The most frustrating part was that I would get questions **all the time** about my heritage and about my face. I never could figure out why those were the first things people wanted to know more about.

At least on that day in the playground, I'd only had to deal with one question.

Back inside, the classroom was cool, bright, and colourful art covered the walls. It gave me a sense of security. As we settled back into our seats, my teacher clapped to get our attention.

'Special announcement!' he said, 'We're going to have a contest!' The room quietened. He had our attention!

'Next week, you'll each get a turn to come up in front of the class and read a passage out of a book. Then everyone will vote on who they think did the best job.'

The class burst into lively chatter. I completely forgot about what had just happened outside. We were being asked to perform! I loved performing! I had taken ballet classes and danced on stage since I was three years old, but I had never delivered a dramatic reading. It felt like a new world was opening up. I started mentally listing every book I owned. My friend poked me.

'What are you going to read? I don't know what book to pick!'

'I don't know either,' I said, 'but I'm going to start practising right away!'

My spirits were high again. When the final bell rang, I packed up as fast as I could. I couldn't wait to tell Mom!

Outside the school, Mom pulled up in our little silver Toyota. I climbed into the back seat.

'How was school today?' she asked cheerfully.

'It was great!' I said. I chattered on about the reading contest for the rest of the drive. Back home in the kitchen, Mom put a plastic blue cup filled with orange juice in front of me and went over to the sink to wash some dishes. The questions continued.

'What did you have for lunch?'

'Chicken fingers!'

'Did you have art today?'

'Yeah! I painted a sunset!'

'What did you do at break time?'

'Played on the bars.'

I took a sip of juice. Then I froze. A dark pit opened in my stomach. It all came flooding back.

Oh no.

I didn't want to remember what had happened.

I looked down at the cup in my hands, swirling the cold juice in a circle. I fell silent. I didn't hear what Mom asked next.

It was as if I had left the room. In my mind, I was back on the playground reliving the whole scene. The hot sun. The feeling of helplessness. The way everything seemed to stand still. From far away, I heard Mom calling my name.

Out of nowhere, I blurted out, 'One of the kids came up to me and wanted to see my tongue. And then she screamed when I showed her.' Tears filled my eyes. Mom shut off the water and turned to look at me.

'I just don't know why it matters,' I said, my words coming out in a wail. 'I feel like an alien! I just want to be normal!' I banged my cup down on the table, pushing it away.

Mom walked over from the sink, her face soft. She looked like she was feeling everything I was feeling. She placed a chair next to mine and gathered me in for a full-body hug.

'Come here,' she said, 'You **are** normal. You're a normal kid just like everyone else. You just have some extra challenges.' I buried my head in her chest. She was a slender woman. My cheek always fitted neatly into the nook right below her collar bone. I breathed in her perfume. My hand found a piece of her shirt. I rubbed the soft fabric between my fingers.

She always told me that I was normal. I knew I wasn't. Normal kids weren't seen as scary. Normal kids didn't have to spend summer break getting surgery. Normal kids didn't hunt for Easter eggs with drainage tubes coming out of their heads.

'I'm **not** normal,' I sobbed, 'I just don't want people to be mean.'

'You know,' she continued, 'the kids that say and do mean things are probably not happy. Maybe their home life is hard. Or maybe their parents haven't taught them how to be kind. That doesn't make it OK, but maybe it may make you feel better to feel sorry for them. Just remember . . . you are so loved.'

I sniffled back a snot bubble. 'I know – **sniff** – you love me – **hiccup** – but I want other people to love me, too.' Mom handed me a tissue and I blew my nose.

'There are a lot of people in your life that love you,' she said softly. 'Don't let anyone dim your light – just be yourself.'

I hugged Mom for a little longer and nodded my head in agreement. I still didn't agree with her insistence that I was 'normal', but I knew she was just trying to be supportive. I headed to the living room. On sad days like this, I liked to dance and disappear into my imagination. Dance was life – though it was hard to dance when my face was in pain, or I was healing from surgery. Mom was so protective during those times. She would make me rest as much as possible while I healed, which meant no dance lessons for a while. But I would always manage to sneak in a quick arabesque or piqué turn in the kitchen, and I never stopped walking on my toes around the house.

Dance took me to other worlds. When I danced, I felt beautiful. When I danced, I felt powerful. When I danced, I felt I could be **anything I wanted**. My go-to was pretending to be the swan princess, Odette, from *Swan Lake*.

I walked over to the tall, boxy stereo and blasted *Swan Lake's* finale music. I spun and leapt about, burning my bare toes as I dragged them across the shaggy brown carpet. I took great care to avoid the dining room table, the couch and the old piano. Well, mostly. I loved to jump off the couch so that it felt like I was flying. I imagined being costumed in a white tutu with a crown of feathers and sparkling diamonds on my head. I loved acting out the final dramatic moments. I ended by melting into a tragic puddle on the ground for the last note of the piece. Then, I rose from the floor and took a deep curtsy. In my fantasy, I heard thunderous applause. I stared into the dark theatre as flowers were thrown onto the stage. I basked in the adoration. I wanted this in real life. Maybe someday I would be in the spotlight, and everyone would love me.

***

A week later, my classmates and I poured into the classroom for the start of school. Today was the reading contest! We were all buzzing. Books flew out of backpacks. We all began practising under our breath. It was showtime!

I had selected a scene from *Matilda* where Miss Trunchbull is screaming at Amanda Thripp, a little girl with pigtails. It was **dramatic**. My favourite! When it came to my turn, I got up from my desk and walked confidently to the front of the classroom. I flipped through the softcover novel to my bookmark, folding the pages backwards. The book bent easily in my sweaty hands. I took a deep breath, and in my mind, transported myself into Matilda's world. I could see the other kids in the yard. I could feel their fear. I tapped into the explosive anger of Miss Trunchbull, holding the book in one hand and gesturing with the other to make myself as big and imposing as possible. My voice boomed.

When I finished, a roar of cheers and applause filled the room. I smiled, pleased, looking down at the floor shyly.

I was in a daze while everyone finished their readings.

'Let's vote quickly before we go on break,' my teacher said.

On small, white slips of paper, we wrote in our votes. I put my head down on my desk. The suspense was too much. Did I have a chance? I started replaying my performance in my head.

Daniela shook my shoulder.

'You won!' she said. I stared at her. I had been a million miles away. Reality slowly came back. I blinked. I blinked again.

Then, it sunk in. '**Yes**!' I was on a cloud.

The bell rang and we headed outside. My friend and I dashed towards the swing set. We weren't the first ones to get there, so we had to wait our turn, but I didn't mind; I was still on my cloud. A few boys from my class gathered behind us to wait their turn, too. A small kid with freckles tapped me on the shoulder.

'Hey! Your eyes are squinty!' he said, using his fingers to pull his eyes into slits. 'Are you **Chinese**?!'

He pressed his hands together in front of him while

shuffling around in a circle and bowing to his friends. He shouted gibberish in an 'Asian' accent. His friends fell about laughing.

I felt like the wind had been knocked out of me, but I didn't say anything. I grabbed a leg of the swing set, gripping the warm metal in my palm. Other kids were turning to look. I didn't want to draw attention to myself. I started to sit down when my friend grabbed my hand.

'Come on, let's go to the bars instead,' she said, glaring at the boys. Then she whispered in my ear, 'Just ignore them.'

We ran off. Behind us, the kid just carried on. He didn't notice we'd left. It felt so strange to have been so happy one minute, and then completely destroyed the next.

When break time ended, one of my classmates came over and congratulated me on winning the contest, edging me back towards that happy feeling again. All of these emotions were very exhausting.

Back at home, Mom poured me some juice and started cooking dinner. She prepared a roast in a big pan as we chatted about the day. I couldn't stop talking about winning the contest. I was too excited. When she asked about break time, I paused. That pit in my stomach opened back up. I told her about the boy and all his friends.

'I don't get it,' I said, squeezing the cup in my hands, 'I won the reading contest and that kid **still** made fun of me.'

Mom popped the roast in the oven and sat down across the table. She looked directly into my eyes. 'Baby girl, no matter what you do, no matter **how good** you are, people will always find **something** to bring you down. That's never going to stop.'

'So even if I become a star ballerina, people will still be mean?' I asked.

She reached for my hand. 'Yep. Mean people will always exist. Don't let them win. Love yourself. No one can take that from you.'

I didn't love myself. How could I when I was just so **weird?!** Maybe someday . . . someday in the far future, I would learn to find that love.

I called Daniela. 'Want to come over?' I asked.

'OK!' she said, 'be right there!'

Daniela never made me feel like I was different. I felt like I could be myself around her. When she got to my house, we ran to the backyard and laughed and played until Mom called us in for dinner.

***

As I grew up, I kept my old friends and found new ones who accepted me for who I was. I tried to ignore bullies and brush aside rude comments. I wasn't always successful. I'm still not always successful. Most of the time, it still stings. I learned a valuable lesson: that being 'normal' meant fitting into a very tiny box that was not built for me. I was never going to have blonde hair and blue eyes. I was never going to have a typical face or an uncomplicated brain, or be free of physical pain. I knew all along: I was **never** going to be a white, non-disabled person's version of 'normal'. So, I went about building my quirky, completely-not-normal life on my own terms. I still live with vascular malformations in my face (those are the medical terms for my conditions), and I'm at peace with it. And through the years, I began to feel strength and pride in being Japanese American, instead of trying to be something I was never meant to be.

While Mom could never understand everything I was feeling, this is the thing she nailed: once I stopped running away from the things that made me **me** . . . once I started focusing on loving my 'weird' self, I did begin to feel better. I stopped trying to 'fix' myself. I started to find others like me. I stopped feeling like I needed to impress other people just to gain their love. It's a long, never-ending journey.

And, I'll never forget that powerful feeling I got from dancing in my living room or reading in front of my class. In fact, when I grew up, I traded my living room and classroom for circus tents, theatres and stadiums. That's right: I became a professional circus artist. I flipped and flew through the air for a living; I entertained thousands of people around the world – and I loved it! More recently, I've started a grassroots endeavour called The FaceOut Project, where I am focusing my attention on gathering and empowering the global Facial Difference community so that, together, we can change hearts and minds, collectively working towards a truly inclusive world.

Wheels on Ice

by Jan Grue

Norway

Was there a moment in time when I came to think of myself as disabled?

In one way, it felt gradual. My muscles did not grow the way my body grew, so while I got taller, I also got weaker.

It was a little like swimming against the waves. I learned to do new things: reading, writing, building ever more complicated structures out of Lego. But every year there were the things that became more difficult for me to do, or that I could no longer do at all. I could walk, but I couldn't run, and getting up off the floor became difficult and then impossible.

I got my first wheelchair at eight. I loved it from the beginning. It had a powerful electric engine and controls that looked like those of a tractor, and I could ride it and it made me less exhausted. So, it was like I was swimming, and mostly keeping my head above water. But then suddenly a big wave would crash over me. And this could happen very suddenly.

There was a green near my elementary school, the Fairy Tale Green. A space meant for ball games, lined with trees and bushes, and these bushes were large enough to hide us and become secret tunnels.

Those hidden spaces were important to us, because the grown-ups couldn't go there. They were very important to me, because I usually had an adult watching me, taking care of me. There were few hidden spaces in my life.

I could climb the small slopes up to the bushes, and then I couldn't.

I could walk for hundreds of metres, and then I couldn't.

I could still ride my wheelchair around the Fairy Tale Green, but it couldn't go into the bushes either. One day, my friends went **up there** to play and I was **down here** and I could not follow them. I could not make them come back to me, and I cried.

That was a strong wave. A crushing wave.

In winter, the bushes and trees that encircled the Fairy Tale Green were dusted with white. The tunnels became snow caves. The central space was flooded with water and turned into an ice rink.

Skating was something I could never do. The muscles in my calves and thighs couldn't support me atop two thin slivers of metal, no more than they could help me run or crouch or leap.

Winter was always my least favourite season, because there was too little to do, too little I **could** do, especially with other children. And winter in Norway is long.

During the winter when I was in fourth grade, a girl in my class sent invitations for her birthday party. It was to start outdoors, on the ice rink. It felt like another wave was about to crash down on me.

But my wheelchair was new to me and I was still learning what it could be, what it and I could do together.

Very carefully I drove it onto the rink. The ice was slippery, but the wheels still had some traction as long as I kept moving.

Then, gaining confidence, I discovered I couldn't just ride the wheelchair the way I normally did. On the ice, I could slide and swerve and suddenly turn, brake and spin. The wheelchair did what I wanted it to do. It was still a strain, managing the long, angled left-hand lever that set the speed, using my right hand to pull and push the shorter lever that steered the wheels. But **fun!** It felt like a strange new kind of freedom.

And then something else happened. One of the other children (who, I wonder?) grabbed on to the back of the wheelchair and was pulled swiftly across the ice. And then someone else grabbed onto **that** child, and another one, and another one . . .

Very soon I had a trail of children hanging on behind me, a comet with a serpentine tail, making impossible manoeuvres, seeing how far I could go, under a frozen starry sky, wishing it would last forever.

Suddenly the wheelchair stopped dead. The long tail of children hanging on had strained the motor until something broke.

I learned two things that day. The first lesson was that when everything clicked, when everything flowed, it could feel as though an object, even a large and heavy machine, was an extension of my body. And when everything flowed, when the wheelchair moved in perfect time, it didn't matter all that much if I was skating or driving. I was moving with the others, and that was what mattered.

The second lesson I learned was that I was still vulnerable in a way that the others weren't. My body was still my body, and that body could get stuck, and I would need help.

Help that day came from the birthday girl's father, who put me in the sidecar of his motorcycle and ferried me to the indoor party, the cake and the candy. I did not think much about my wheelchair, lifeless and stuck on the ice, and what my parents would do to bring it home, to have it repaired. I was still a child; those tasks came later. It didn't yet feel like I'd left a part of my body behind.

And for the rest of that night, and for a long time afterwards, I only remembered what it had meant to have that comet's tail of children hanging on to me, and to be lost in that moment.

This wheelchair, the Permobil, the one that could very nearly pull a whole class of children along the ice, set a high bar. Over the years I came to know many others. Smaller powered chairs that were better at turning sharp corners, lighter manual wheelchairs that could be folded up and placed in the trunk of a car.

As I grew up, those wheelchairs allowed me to visit new places, to learn new lessons. With two travelling companions, I once spent a very long afternoon on the outskirts of Moscow looking for, and failing to find, a bicycle repair shop, because I had gone to Russia without a single spare tyre.

It was a strange way to think about my body, always connected to the world, but it rang true, and sometimes it connected me to other people in unexpected ways. Years later, a large and very kind Samoan man pushed me all the way through San Francisco Airport, because the cheap chair I'd rented to go to Chicago had quietly emptied out its battery during the flight back.

I always kept a Permobil; I still do. It is my strongest and most capable body, the one that can follow forest trails and climb steep hills. It is big and a little clunky, even though the manual controls have been replaced by power steering, and the long, angled stick for the gas has turned into a neat little four-way joystick. Highly charged, able to leap off at high speed – I even smacked it into a tree once, overcome with the joy of rapid movement.

It felt like magic, nothing to do with being 'wheelchair-bound'. And at some point, a few years after I'd become a writer, I thought: **Why not? Why not embrace the magic?** And so I wrote a children's book called *Oliver*, where an inventor wanted to build something so that his son could move around in the world, but tried and failed to come up with the right idea.

A chair on metal springs, bouncing around the house?

A chair hanging from balloons, powered by a great big fan?

Mechanical trousers, coal-fired and red-hot?

These were different bodies, spectacular and impractical, but magical – and good for riding out the waves. I even thought of a dolphin-powered water chair, one that could actually surf the waves, and though I don't expect to have one any time soon, I still love the image.

Finally, the inventor and his son found a pack of living wheelchairs. They were creatures of the sun-drenched plains, feeding on iron ore, dreading a spiky monster called the Odradek, which punctured their tyres. They caught one, tamed it, they loved it and it loved them, and they learned to build a machine that could do the same things that it could.

And that is how the wheelchairs came into the world: a bit of invention, a bit of magic.

I didn't become a father until five years after I wrote that book, but it feels, now, like it was a way to prepare. A way to make wheelchairs into something wondrous. Not something to make people avert their eyes.

I say 'people', but I mean 'adults'. Kids already know that wheelchairs are magical. In kindergarten, when my son and I came through the gates, every child that could move on their own instantly swarmed us.

'Is that a car?'

'What does that button do?'

'You can't go inside the house, that's a car.'

'Can I ride with you?'

'Can I drive it?'

A little car that is allowed to go inside the house. The magic was there all along.

As I grew older, I didn't feel the waves as strongly. And at times I thought, **this is it, I've learned what there is to know about disability**. But that was never right, because time doesn't stop – I grow older, the people I love grow older, and the world is changing all around us.

Maybe the waves just feel softer because I've gotten used to them. Like on the North Shore of Oahu, in Hawaii, where I saw children learning to jump and roll when the crest came nearer, moving with the water. It is a skill that comes with knowing both your body and your surroundings, knowing where you are in the world – and what the world can offer.

On another beach, in Barcelona, my wife, myself and our son saw for the first time a wheelchair that could go into the water. Three big wheels on a plastic frame, and we could all swim together in the Mediterranean Sea.

The next year, we found that they make electric folding wheelchairs now, small enough to go in the trunk of the car, and we realised: **we can go everywhere**.

The vulnerability doesn't go away, though. In a museum in Berlin on a very hot day, the elevators stopped working and we were stuck on one of the exhibition floors. Still, I could drive slowly around the floor looking, and my son could fall asleep on my lap.

Every time I send the Permobil off into the hold of an aeroplane, I am letting go of a body part, hoping it will come back unharmed. My family know this. We feel the same joy when we see it again. It belongs to my body and we belong to each other; this is how we are in the world.

We are still figuring everything out. We will always be figuring it out.

The year our son turned five years old, winter was cold
and dry. There was not much snow, but the ice rinks
in Oslo were full of people – the big one downtown,
where the lights that go up before Christmas were still
shining, and the small ones all around the city, changed
from soccer pitches and baseball courts into crystal
smoothness.

I didn't live near the Fairy Tale Green anymore, but there
was another ice rink near our house, in a tiny valley
surrounded by tall apartment buildings. One day, the
three of us went out carrying two pairs of skates, and my
son sat on a bench, his legs dangling, while my wife tied
on his skates for the first time.

She held his arms as they wobbled over to the rink, and
continued to hold him as he tried a few careful steps,
unfamiliar with the new way he had to move. He was
nervous of falling down, and it was all strange – the
slippery surface, the stiff tall shoes.

I saw it, I could call out words of encouragement, but
I couldn't do what she was doing, holding him and
guiding. I wanted to be with him, to feel his body close,
because that is the most important thing a parent

129

can do: be there.

And then I remembered something. I drove my wheelchair onto the rink, and told him that he could grab on to the back of it, which he did. There was only him, but I felt a strange echo of the birthday party many years ago, the long tail of children trailing me on the ice.

At first I drove very, very slowly, and then a tiny bit faster, pulling him along the ice, looking over my shoulder every few seconds, and finding, every time, that we were smiling at each other.

Dear Carly

by Carly Findlay

Australia

Dear Little Carly,

I'm remembering you at twelve years old.

You've lived with a rare, severe skin condition called
ichthyosis all of your life. It means you have scaly red
skin, and it affects the whole of your body. You're
just starting to take care of it without the help of your
parents; you know the deal with applying ointments and
seeing a handful of specialists. Even though you've got a
handle on the medical stuff, the social aspects are really
hard to manage. The constant stares and questions
get you down. It's hard being ridiculed and excluded.
And you just want to look like everyone else. But not
even your mum's Clinique will cover up ichthyosis.

You've just started high school. Mum said you would
have a different time at high school compared to
primary school, in terms of making friends, but I know
it feels pretty similar to you. The kids are still scared of

sitting next to you in case they catch something. You are lucky to be able to spend a lot of time in the school library; books are your escape.

At twelve, you are still tiny. Mum bought you a school uniform so big that it will last you until you finish year ten. So embarrassing. At least your socks are the cool slouchy ones, designed to effortlessly concertina up the ankle. Some kids at school have an undercut – a shaved scalp under their hair. Your hair is always sparse, you're embarrassed that your silly scalp means you too have an undercut of sorts, because your brittle hair breaks off.

You've been reading *TV Hits* magazine for years, cutting up the song lyrics each month, alphabetising them in a pile and securing them with a rubber band. I know you're so proud of this pile, and your ability to memorise song lyrics. This pile is the neatest thing in your very untidy bedroom. Recently, you've started to read *Dolly* and *Girlfriend* magazines, too – the two main Australian mags for teenage girls. Every girl at school is reading them. Cover girls are white women, sometimes famous, but often 'girl next door' modelling competition winners too. Kids at school enter these competitions but discourage you from doing so. This discouragement only further confirms the othering and isolation that you've felt since you realised you were different to other kids. Even playing with Mum's Clinique make-up samples won't make you look like them. Your red, scaly skin will still exist underneath.

Really, Mum should ban those magazines for their ridiculous beauty standards, which I know contribute to you feeling like a freak. Those articles tell teenage girls how to get the perfect skin to attract the perfect guy – only, your skin is not like anyone else's in *Dolly* or *Girlfriend*, which, to you, confirms you'll never have a boyfriend. Or girlfriend. Adverts for acne wash and pink razors convince you that you need them. But, Carly, you don't have any acne and you have zero body hair. I advise you to stop dragging Dad's (unused) razor up those hairless legs of yours, otherwise you'll get another skin infection!

Summer sport in your first year of high school is swimming. You can't do swimming, so you get to choose an indoor sport with the older kids. You choose roller-skating, at the Village Rink. The soundtrack is the same every week – mostly eighties music with a few new songs in the mix. In the future, you'll think of speed skating at the Village every time 'Real Wild Child' by Iggy Pop comes on the radio.

I know at your first skate session, just last week, you met the boy you'll be crushing on for two years. You're slow but confident on skates, but while you were skating to Bryan Adams' 'Summer of '69' you felt something strange happen to your left skate, like a wheel was working its way loose. Suddenly a boy, one year older than you, glided up to you on his sleek black rollerblades – definitely not hired from the rink! Your hire skate's wheel had come off, and this dreamboat was here to save you. He had shoulder-length blond hair and a wide smile, as cool as any boy in *Dolly* magazine. He smiled and handed you the wayward wheel, and he let you hook your arm around his to get off the rink safely. Carly, his name is Adam, and you are in love.

So here's how you're going to play it. You'll play it cool. Week after week, that's all you'll do. You'll never have a proper conversation beyond that first engagement; you'll just exchange 'hellos'. You'll refer to him as 'Ahem' to the few friends that you have, because you don't want anyone knowing your crush's name. If anyone got wind of your crush's identity, you know they'd tease both you and him. The crush has to stay in your imagination, because based on what you've learned in magazines, a boy like him would never go for a girl like you.

Carly, soon you'll miss a fair bit of school because of your skin. Hospital stays always feel like a reprieve for you because the other kids on the ward understand what it's like to be sick, even if they don't have the same disability as you. You will develop strong friendships with these kids, and the nurses too. However, the hardest thing about being a patient with a rare medical condition is the medical conferences. I know you've been doing these since you were six – pitched to you as an opportunity for doctors to find a cure by looking at your skin, but I also know it's weighing you down. There are always doctors from all around the world at these conferences. Some just look at you, without even speaking to you. At these conferences you are freezing, sitting in the hospital room wearing just your undies and one sock (the doctors really have to look at your feet!). At this point, your breasts are starting to bud, and you're self-conscious too. I know you're starting to feel like you can't do this anymore, that you're sick of being a medical exhibit. And I know you're thinking about saying this to Mum and Dad. You should say it, Carly. Don't worry, they'll listen to you, and, after that, you'll be able to keep your body to yourself.

Would you like to know more about your future? In a few

years, when your school dress finally sits above the knee, you'll develop a huge obsession with the band Savage Garden. This will lead to lifelong fandom. At high school, you will develop a strong friendship with another Savage Garden fan, which finally makes you feel like you're a part of a group at school. You'll dub VHS tapes so that you each have copies of Savage Garden on *Jay Leno*, and you'll sneakily use the school library to search for Savage Garden on the internet. Your fandom will consume you. Years later, Savage Garden's frontman Darren Hayes will tell you 'what makes you different is what sets you apart' and you'll never forget this.

The stern school librarian will discourage you from searching for Savage Garden and, instead, she will suggest you look up ichthyosis. You may think she's just being strict, but much later you'll realise she knows how alone you feel, and that she wants to see you connect with others who understand what you're going through. It'll feel like you're being told off, but it's her way of showing you love. She's pushing you towards finding a disability community. And you will, Carly. You'll find an ichthyosis message board, and you'll realise you aren't alone: there are others out there, like you. You will have waited so many years for this.

In the future, your parents will be strict. You already know they're strict, even though you're a straight-laced kid who gets good grades, and that isn't going to change even when you continue to do well at school – and even when you don't get drunk until you're twenty-three! They won't let you listen to Alanis Morissette because of the swearing and relationship references, and they'll steer your education towards a 'sensible' university course that you'll hate, so you'll get a 'sensible' government job that you'll stick with for fifteen years. This will be difficult, but they'll do all this because they love you, and because you're the first in their families to reach such a high level of education. Later, you'll learn this is part of being a child to migrant parents – they sacrificed so much by moving to Australia, and so many of your friends who are also children of migrants will say they had a similar experience. But please know that it is OK to follow your own path, to grow up and be your own person, even if that's a different person to the one your parents imagined.

In many years' time, a move from your tiny home town to Melbourne will open your mind and give you so many opportunities, Carly. You'll study media and work on your writing as a side hustle at night after your government job – this will be your passion. And you'll be speaking on many stages – at the Sydney Opera House, in Bali and in the UK – focusing on disability rights, access and inclusion, and how, for you, disability now means community, cultural identity and pride. Standing on stages in front of so many people will be a world away from not wanting to be looked at, which is (I know) how you feel right now.

Your parents will be proud of you, whatever you do, even if it's not what they'd choose for themselves, and even if Dad doesn't tell you so very often. You'll write a book in the future, and Mum will carry it around with her everywhere. She'll even show it to the Conservative prime minister at the Country Women's Association conference – he's not really your target audience, but could do with reading about disability rights!

When you're in your thirties, you'll really start living. That's almost two decades away – but I promise that you'll be thriving, so hang on in there. You'll have incredible friends, be a published writer and take up roller-skating again. You'll marry a funny and kind man who finds joy in your skin. But marriage won't be your greatest achievement. Your greatest achievement will be finding love for yourself, and accepting your skin and facial difference, after so many years of wanting to be like those girls in *Dolly* and *Girlfriend* magazines. It will be such a relief!

You'll find out it's so much easier to love yourself than to hate yourself.

Your hair will never be thick, but it will curl past your shoulders, after you find the right (respectful!) hairdressers, and you commit to conditioning it every day.

You'll wear incredibly colourful clothes – people will stop you in the street, telling you they love your dress, instead of asking you if you've been sunburned.

You'll use social media to educate others. You'll be in magazines and on TV. You'll change the media for people with ichthyosis so they'll see themselves represented. And high school kids (and adults) will google ichthyosis and find you online, like when you searched for ichthyosis as a teen. Imagine that!

You'll even be in your school hall of fame – your photo hanging up alongside someone who bullied you!

One night in the future, you'll be at a restaurant and a

twelve-year-old girl will come up to you and ask: 'Excuse me, are you **the** Carly Findlay?' And you'll giggle shyly and say yes, inviting her for a selfie.

So, hang in there, twelve-year-old Little Carly, the world's not ready for you yet. But it will be, just you wait.

Lip-reading in Odesa

by Ilya Kaminsky

Ukraine (Former USSR)

The USSR, the country we live in, is about to fall apart, but no one knows this yet. I am a twelve-year-old deaf boy and outside, in the streets, we are playing War. A three-year-old girl is a nurse. She is saving us under bombardment. But we are surrounded. Eleven wooden rifles are raised and aimed at her. She protects her eyes from the snow with one hand, crosses the porch, goes down three steps, approaches the pavement, and stops in front of the bakery. The wooden gun barrels haven't lost sight of her for an instant.

'Hello, boys,' she smiles.

Kids are playing War: I watch a four-year-old soldier's hand tremble as he presses a wooden gun to my three-year-old neighbour's back. They walk. Whenever someone approaches, the tiny soldier stops.

Kids are playing War: I am putting my hands to the wall and hear a gunshot, two gunshots, an imaginary truck is on imaginary fire. I take my hands off the wall, nothing.

I put my hands back on the wall – four seven-year-old soldiers are on patrol. They have drawn patchy little beards with ink on their jaws. They laugh at each other. Stick out their chests.

We are playing War: our bellies are the drums on which we tap the national anthem. Our fingers are the flags. Across the courtyard, little boys line up along the wall, waiting for war.

***

At first, there is fear. I am a boy walking home from school when a Jewish woman pushes past the crowds of kids coming out of the building and shoves a photograph to my face.

Her lips move, frantically.

'I can't hear you,' I say.

I point to my ears.

I see her turn to another Jewish-looking kid, then to another.

She asks them a question, but I only see the most exaggerated motions of her face. She turns to another kid nearby.

'Have you seen my daughter?'

She turns away and hurries on, before I can see anything but her question.

We are both stunned and not.

***

Alongside the fear, life around us is going on, as if nothing is happening. On our balcony, in chestnut branches, my father is teaching me how to read lips. We are aiming binoculars at old ladies gossiping on the bench across the yard. Behind them, the children are playing War.

And I just want to watch, a breathless watch: lips of postman, of third-floor housewife, lips munching on gooseberries, lips of boys who are stealing a fistful of currants from an old lady's bag as she gossips on the bench.

I see the lips of an older girl who counts on her fingers as two other girls kiss: eight, nine, ten, eleven. I am watching how the language taps their cheeks and noses, how they navigate their lips between sounds of dogs' yelps and grandmothers' sneezes, and how behind them they leave the clicks of heels.

I am learning to hear with my eyes.

In the chestnut branches, my father and I, like two thieves, watch our people's lips.

The truth is, no one yet knows what is about to happen to us.

We do not yet know that the country will fall apart. We do not yet understand what's about to happen.

***

I am a twelve-year-old deaf boy when a man laughs at me on a public bus when I say that I write poetry.

Impossible! How can anyone deaf even know what poetry **is**?

At home, I ask my father: What is poetry?

Father does what he always does – he tells a story.

He says, once, a deaf man asked his wife to sit at the piano and play as loudly as possible the entire repertoire of Chopin. And while she slapped the keys, he dropped onto his hands and knees . . . and bit into the piano's wood.

And that . . .

My father paused. He didn't have to go on. I understood.

But he went on:

That is poetry.

Most of the stories I hear from my father are about war. Past wars. In his stories, it is 1941. He is shaved so that Germans won't notice his dark hair, won't know that he is Jewish. He is learning to dance. The woman – Natalia – who hides my father, hides him for three years, from 1941 to 1944. Not an easy task to keep a restless child inside for three years. Natalia teaches him how to tango.

They dance, for three years of that war, in the room where curtains are always drawn, for three years of occupation, an old woman and a child.

Once, he escapes outside to play and the German soldiers see him, so he runs to the market and hides behind boxes of tomatoes. (Now, as an adult, and a poet, all my friends tell me there are too many tomatoes in my poems. They say there is too much dancing. Can there ever be too much dancing? I am not sure.)

This is what I know: in the middle of a war – an aged woman and a shaved child tango in a dark apartment.

Then, the war ends and there is no food. Natalia buys a pack of cigarettes, sells them at the train station, one cigarette at a time.

It is February. She walks between wagons, an eight-year-old holding the side of her coat. 'Cigarettes,' he yells. 'Cigarettes!'

My father bends to tie his shoes, and his story stops because I cannot see his lips. He straightens up, and the story continues. That is how it is for a lip-reading boy's storytelling time.

***

So, what is poetry?

It is a language of senses and passion.

For me, a poem is a spell.

Not just a spell about an event, but something that becomes an event in and of itself.

Years ago, my father told me a story of a man who, when he couldn't hear, got down on all fours and bit into a piano leg, so he could hear the music with his teeth.

The language of poetry speaks to all our senses, my father meant to say.

It can speak, privately, to all of us.

It is visceral.

I cannot come back to the past, but a poem's language can open a room where the past still exists.

And that, I think, is magic.

All Bodies Are Good Bodies

by Nina Tame

United Kingdom

'What's got two legs and a hump? . . . Nina!'

As far as jokes go, that is a bloomin' rubbish one because, well, basically, it's just **facts**. I do indeed have two legs and I do indeed have a hump (I call it my lump) on my back. Hi, I'm Nina, the two-legged-hump person. I was born a long, long time ago, way back in the 1980s when we didn't have mobile phones and our tellies only had four channels. This may sound like a terrible way to live but we did have a cartoon called *Count Duckula*, which was about a vegetarian vampire duck; and you could get sweets for a penny; and for some reason, the orange and blue Smarties in a tube just tasted way better in the eighties than they do now. So, I still think we had it pretty good.

I was born in Essex to Barb and Dave (that's my mum and dad), and I grew up with my big sister Weise (Louise to everyone else), and Mark, my big brother. I was born disabled with a condition called spina bifida, which essentially means the nerves in my spine are a lil' jumbled up and live inside a lump on my lower back. I use a wheelchair these days, and I'm missing a few toes now, too, but that wasn't the case when I was a kid – back then, you wouldn't have even known I was disabled unless you saw the lump on my back.

I didn't think I was different from anyone else, and I didn't really think about the lump on my back either – no more than I thought about my elbows or my knees. It was just a part of me like all the other parts. For the first six years of my life, I didn't feel different from anyone else at all. Not until someone pointed out that I was.

Summer 1986, Stacy Thompson's house

Stacy Thompson lived across the street from us and a little bit along. We weren't really friends, but I think my ma was friends with her ma and I'd get dragged along when they met up for a natter – you know how it is. Stacy Thompson had the best toys, though. Not only did she have a Barbie Dreamhouse, but she also had a Mr Frosty; and lemme tell you, Mr Frosty was **the** toy of the eighties. Imagine getting to have slushies on tap wherever you wanted them. I was well impressed.

She also had a brilliant dressing-up box. Her ma used to

make homemade costumes of whatever Stacy wanted. I thought that was the coolest thing ever because it meant we could play a game of Transformers vs ThunderCats and look the part, and that's exactly what we decided to do.

I was just taking my T-shirt off, ready to get into a leotard and turn into Cheetara (my favourite ThunderCat), when I heard Stacy say, 'Ewww, what's that?!' I poked my head back out of my top to see what Stacy was making a big fuss about, and she was staring and pointing right at me. Oh no! Did I have a massive bogey on my face? Had I trodden in dog poo? What was she pointing at?

Oh, it was my lump.

I didn't really know what my lump was at that point. My folks had never sat me down and been like: 'Now, Nina, we need to talk about the lump on your back.' It was just my lump. So, I didn't know what to say to Stacy who was still staring at me with her nose scrunched up, like there was actual dog poo in the room with us. I didn't know my body like I do now. I didn't have the words to say, 'Oh, this cool thing? This is my lump – it was a free gift when I was born, and it keeps all my nerves from my spine safe and sound inside it.' And because I didn't have those words, I just mumbled something like: 'Oh, it's just my lump,' and I carried on getting changed.

That was the first time I'd ever felt embarrassed about my body. It was the first time I'd ever wanted the ground to swallow me whole or longed to be instantly teleported back to the safety of my house. From that day on, I thought about my body a bit more. I thought about my lump, and I thought it must be gross.

The trickiest thing was the fact that no one told me any different. You see, I didn't tell anyone about what Stacy said; I just sort of tucked it away into a box inside my brain marked Embarrassing Things. My mum and dad never spoke about my lump either; same way they never spoke about my knees or my elbows. The only time my lump was mentioned was in my yearly hospital check-ups when a doctor would poke and prod it and then I'd be sent on my merry way.

1990, Primary School PE

When I got to secondary school, PE was essentially a lesson I never took because I spent most of that time on crutches. Before that, though, I was well into PE. In primary school I was on the hockey and netball teams, and I loved doing both. However, the school changing rooms were a different story, especially when Fiona Arnold was around.

Fiona was mean. She was mean to everyone except her two besties, who weren't quite as mean but always giggled along when Fiona was demolishing her latest target, which, on this day, in those tiny changing rooms surrounded by the whole hockey team, was me.

***

There I was, getting changed, when Fiona sneaked a peek from behind me and loudly yelled: 'Nina's got a lump on her back!' Her minions giggled and shrieked and said, 'Eww, Nina's a camel!' Fiona was gleefully overjoyed at this and looked positively triumphant when she said: 'What's got two legs and a hump? . . . Nina!'

That was her rubbish factual 'joke'.

Urghhh. What should we wish on bullies? Holes in their socks for eternity? May their toast always land butter side down? May the other side of their pillow always be warm? Ooooh, have you ever had a choc dip? It's a small pot of chocolate with little biscuit fingers for dipping. They are the best thing ever and used to be my number-one pick at the sweet shop. Well, I once bought one using my pocket money, peeled back the lid, and it had **zero** biscuit fingers. I was robbed. May every person who has ever laughed at the way someone else looks have zero biscuits in their choc dips, and holey socks forever.

By the time I was a teenager, I'd broken various bones in my feet, so I had to wear orthopaedic shoes which I **hated**, and I used crutches on and off a lot. I couldn't hide my disability like I used to. I mean, I still kept my lump hidden, but the rest of my differences were pretty obvious. It wasn't all bad – I had some really sweet friends but there were also some really mean friends, and I didn't have any friends who were different in the way I was. I didn't know anyone disabled like me. So, I continued to try to shove my disability and every mean thing anyone had ever said about it away in that box marked Embarrassing Things. Only, it was getting pretty full.

And that's how I grew up: believing that my disabled parts were gross and wrong and something to be hidden when they weren't at all. I grew up thinking there were rules about how a body should look because a lot of the grown-ups, and a lot of the people on the telly, and basically everyone else, were always talking about how a body should look, and no one ever spoke about a disabled body like mine.

You're probably wondering how long it took me to realise that my disability wasn't something I should be hiding, aren't you? Want to guess? Five years? Ten years? I wish. Let's fast-forward twenty-three years. Yes, I was 31.

September 2013, a hospital in Essex

I'd just had a baby. A baby boy. My third kiddo and he's got spina bifida just like me. He's got freckles that scatter across his cheeks like stars, and the softest lump on his lower back. I think both are beautiful. Hold on now, though, because if I think his lump is beautiful, then surely that means that mine is too? **Holy macaroni, Batman** – are you telling me for all these years I just presumed Stacy and Fiona were right when, **actually**, they were **wrong**? Excellent news. I wish that news had come a teeeeensy bit sooner.

When I saw my kid's disability, I saw how I'd been told a whopper of a porky pie lie about what bodies should look like. This is a life spoiler for you, and it's a good 'un. Actually, maybe it's more of a life hack. Anyway, buckle up. Hold onto your hats. Drum roll pleeeeease . . . **DUM DUM DUUUUUM** . . . !

There are no rules about what a body should look like!

None. Zero. Zilch.

All bodies are good bodies. All of 'em.

It's silly, really. Do you think that there's only one way a body should look? Do you think that if people think you're 'too fat' or 'too thin' or 'too small' or 'too tall', that if you've got lumps and bumps, or a birthmark on your face, that if you use a wheelchair or wear orthopaedic shoes, or if you have a scar or a missing limb, or if you wear a leg brace, then that difference should be labelled as a Bad Thing? That makes no sense to me now.

These days, I can see how strange it is for people to focus on what someone looks like on the outside. Why does it matter how a person's body works? Shouldn't what's on the inside be more important? After all, it's the least interesting thing about a person, really, what they look like. I wanna know all the important stuff, like their favourite crisps. Mine is probably beef Monster Munch. It was Rib 'n' Saucy Nik Naks for nearly a whole year but then I ate too many and felt a bit sick so we're having a break.

I'm lucky that, as a grown-up, I'm now surrounded by people of all different shapes and sizes. I now have lots of very cool disabled friends, and friends who are different from me in all sorts of other ways, too.

Sometimes, when you're small, your world can be small too, even though it feels really big. You might feel different from the other kids in your class, or your mates in your friend group, and you might think your difference is a Bad Thing. I promise on all the Monster Munch and Nik Naks in the world that it's not.

There are no rules about what a body should look like.

You don't have to hide your body or change your body, and you don't have to love it either. Remember how I said, right at the start of this story, that I didn't used to think about my lump, just like I didn't really think about my elbows or my knees? That it was only other people's comments that made me question that feeling? Well, now I feel like that again – it's not that I don't think about my lump, it's that I view it just like my elbows and my knees.

It's just a part of my body. It's part of what makes me **me**.

And that's enough.

Performance

by Daniel Sluman

United Kingdom

I wasn't one of the popular, confident kids. I loved
reading and learning. In comparison to my friends, I
was a little bit quiet. I had dreams about being in the
limelight, but the thought of too much attention scared
me. Maybe that's why I was goalkeeper.

I loved playing football with my friends, but I wasn't that
fast or skilled. I couldn't dribble past two defenders in
a moment or score goals from incredible angles. So, I
went in goal. Goalkeeper was the last position anyone
wanted, so I always got to play, and because I worked
hard and jumped for every save, I managed to win a
little popularity in my own way. I might not have scored
the winning goal but sometimes I made the winning
save, jumping like a cat and plucking the ball out of
mid-air.

So, I had some attention, but not too much. Which is
just how I liked it. But then, as I turned eleven, something
happened that changed all that.

***

I still remember the way the tumour looked on the screen: a small round halo of white flakes against the black film, like snow in a snow globe. I'd had this lump on my knee for weeks, but I didn't think it was anything to worry about, just a knock from diving for the ball on the frozen school field. I still remember seeing my mum and dad come out of the doctor's office with tears in their eyes as they explained that the tumour on the screen meant **cancer**. At eleven, I had no idea what that really meant. I just noticed everyone around me starting to look very worried, and suddenly I was away from my friends and my school and the football pitch and in hospital all the time. The chemotherapy they put in my body made me feel sick and so tired that I needed naps during the day. And then after a while my hair started falling out, too.

After a few months of treatment, I had gone almost completely bald from the medicine, and was wearing baseball caps because people had started to point and stare. I was tired and sad with all the travelling, with missing my friends at school, and from the worry my cancer seemed to be causing to everyone who loved me. I still didn't really understand quite how serious things were but everyone around me just looked so afraid. I remember the day when my dad drove us to a hospital in Birmingham where we saw a stern-looking doctor. He picked up the thin slices of black film from my most recent scans and placed them against the light, made some anxious noises, and finally sat us both down to explain what was going on inside me. The medicine they were giving me, the same horrible stuff that made me feel sick and made my hair come out in fistfuls, wasn't working. The tumour in my leg, this big lump near my knee, was getting bigger, and if they didn't do something soon it would spread to the rest of my body, and it could kill me. The only thing they could do to save me was to cut off my left leg.

***

The actual operation and the time around it was a blur. I remember going to sleep surrounded by surgeons and nurses and then waking up with my dad beside me. My left leg was gone, but I couldn't feel anything yet because the drugs they had given me were making me so sleepy; I felt like I was in a dream. After a few days in bed the medication wore off and the nurses made me stand up and learn how to walk around with crutches, moving slowly up the first step in a staircase and back down again until the pain and tiredness made me feel like I might faint. Slowly, I got better at swinging my body between my crutches, my muscles beginning to learn how to carry my weight in this new way, and I was released from hospital.

I tried to get used to my new body while recovering at home. I started to think about my future and the realities of my disability. Football seemed to be finished, for me. I had no idea that amputee football existed – that football with one leg and crutches, as I discovered later, was a thing. And even if I could have learned to play, would I have wanted to?

My amputation was high – all of my left leg was gone, which meant learning to use a prosthesis was going to be difficult. The prosthetic wraps around your waist. It's hot and uncomfortable, and it digs into your hips, so most people like me move around more easily on crutches. But doing that meant I would bring a lot of attention to myself. I knew that every time I walked outside the door I would be stared at and held by the glances of strangers who at best would be curious, at worst, horrified by the way I looked. I was never the most confident child in my class but now I felt so nervous about how I appeared in public and what people would think about me. I was embarrassed just imagining it. I wanted to lock myself away from the world.

Eventually my interests turned from football towards music and learning how to play electric guitar, something I could do entirely in the safety of home. My dad bought me a brand-new guitar from the music shop – it was dark with fiery blue waves and a lot bigger and heavier than I thought it would be. At first it hurt my fingers to stretch them over the metal frets, but after a few weeks' practice it got easier and my hands learned how to move across the neck and find my first few chords.

I spent hours and hours practising my favourite bands' songs, and even when I didn't have the guitar in my hands, I would play music in my room and close my eyes, imagining it was me strumming, picking and bending the notes. In my mind I was performing in front of an audience full of strangers and it didn't feel embarrassing or scary: I wasn't being noticed because of my disability, I was being seen because of my talent. I could do what I wanted most: I could make people feel something magical with my music. But this daydream was also bittersweet. I thought that I would never be able to make it come true, regardless of how good I was or how many thousands of hours I put into practising.

I had never seen anyone with one leg in a band. I had never seen someone with one leg on a stage. I hardly ever saw people with one leg anywhere, except perhaps on TV programmes where they were shrieking in pain on a hospital ward. As time went by, the idea of playing guitar anywhere outside of my bedroom became a secret I kept to myself.

Before my leg was cut off, I really enjoyed classes and loved learning new things, but a few years into high school I felt like each day was the same boring six hours repeated again and again. Now I had been through the rollercoaster of my cancer, school seemed a lot less important to me, and at a time when everyone was worrying about fitting in, I felt resigned that I wouldn't because of the way I looked. I didn't take classes seriously and my grades started getting worse, and none of the subjects spoke to me. I couldn't imagine what kind of career a one-legged man could have that would come from learning at school. At lunchtime all my friends played football like usual, and I stayed in, often by myself, reading. Without sports to keep us together, I drifted away from them and felt more and more isolated outside of classes.

One morning, I heard two boys in my year talking about a band that I loved. I wasn't close to Lucien and Mike, but I had never spoken to anyone who even knew this band (let alone liked them), and so we started talking about our favourite songs. It turned out that, along with Billie and Phil, Mike and Lucien were starting a band and having their first rehearsal at Phil's house. Somehow my lips started moving and I heard the words, 'I play guitar' fall out of my mouth. I have no idea where those words came from! The idea of playing guitar with other people – people who might think I'm awful, people who might think I'm too disabled to be in a band, that I would make the band look silly – was terrifying. I wouldn't have been surprised if they'd mumbled politely and moved back to their conversation, but they smiled and told me where they were rehearsing next week!

My dad gave me a lift to the first rehearsal. I remember nervously tapping my foot in the car and thinking over all the worst possible scenarios: not being good enough, not fitting in, them being afraid to tell me they didn't want me in the band. Beneath all these nerves there was still a small, confident part of me that knew this might just work out: that as long as I could sit comfortably enough to play, there was a chance this might be what I'd been dreaming of.

We were in the garage of Phil's parents' house, and beyond plugging our amps in and getting in tune I don't remember much from the rehearsal except the absolute joy of playing music together. Those few hours were the most fun I'd had in a long time. We even wrote a couple of songs using ideas I had come up with over months of practice at home. Not only was I in the band, but we sounded good. I felt like I was really doing what I was meant to do.

Over the next few months, we rented out the tiny community centre in Lucien's village, and every week our parents helped us haul our amplifiers, guitars and drum kit up to the dusty room filled with stacks of chairs and bibles. Phil kept us all in time on the drums and Billie's bass made the chairs vibrate with fast-fingered lines like snakes slithering on the floor. I came up with a lot of the structure for the songs we were building, and Mike played the coolest and weirdest notes high up on the neck of his guitar. Lucien thought up the words to our songs and sang and shouted and sometimes screamed them, on top of all the rest. Sometimes his parents let us practise in his room and afterwards we would talk together about the kind of songs we wanted to write, what the band should look like, and how one day, we wanted to record a demo. And I was excited about that, but most of all I was so happy just to have these four friends, and to be able to create a shared language together with our instruments.

Everything was going so well. Maybe I should have known where it was going – our first gig.

Once a month the main hall in the town I grew up in was used for live music. Most of my year at school would go there and watch some bands from bigger towns and cities play, often supported by smaller bands from school. The headline acts were always very slick. You could tell they had rehearsed for years and refined their sound, and after the gigs we clamoured for the CDs of their demos that were often for sale out of the back of a car. This town hall would be the first place that our band would play live, in front of friends and family, which made it even more nerve-wracking.

I remember anxiously talking to the people running the show about how I was going to perform. I couldn't comfortably stand while playing, as the guitar was too heavy and I would lose my balance. The only viable choice was to sit on a chair on the stage, so I could play like I did in rehearsal. I was still extremely nervous about all this. A large part of a band performing is visual: the look of the group. As a one-legged guitarist, I was going to stick out, regardless of anything I did. I spent a lot of nights awake in bed, thinking about how I would be received, going through all the worst possibilities.

I can remember how cold it was when we performed. It must have been winter, and frosty outside, but when I walked up the wooden steps to the main room I was hit by the warmth of the people filling up the hall: not just the heat from their bodies in a confined space, but the warm feeling of enthusiasm and encouragement from all the kids there. You could barely find room to get to the stage, shouldering past our friends, past the kids in other friendship groups, past the girls who would hardly speak to us. Everyone was wearing their casual clothes, the jeans and T-shirts and dresses and trainers we would wear every day if we were allowed. It all felt very grown up, with everyone suddenly free to express themselves outside of the imaginary lines that separated us at school.

I climbed up to the dusty stage on my crutches, and flinched at the sharp crackle of feedback when I plugged in my guitar. When we were all ready, I shuffled until I was comfortable in my chair, and looked out into the crowd. The room was packed with faces of people I knew and some I didn't. As Lucien started talking on the mic, I could barely hold my shaking pick between my fingers. I was sure I would mess up at the earliest point. I was sure I would be stared and pointed at by half my school year. Somehow, I got my hand moving in time with the drums as the first song began – the first of these songs that we had been rehearsing for months. It sounded . . . good. Not only that, it also sounded good to the audience. People were moving and nodding along. A few very enthusiastic rock nerds were forming a little mosh pit, where they ran and bumped into each other, in time to our song – this song of ours that I wrote in the first rehearsal, in Phil's garage.

I soon forgot about everything except the music. Between the five of us on stage we were making a hurricane of noise. There were layers of crash cymbals and thickly distorted guitars, pierced by Lucien's wailing and pointed enunciation, with Billie's bass holding the whole tune together underneath it all. What I realised in rehearsals and gigs is that playing in a band means working hard to make this wonderful piece of sound between you. It's not about each of you showing off, it's about helping each other, creating space for everyone to find their voice and explore the limits of their instrument and their personal expression. That night at the town hall, I felt like we were playing better than we ever had.

I had no idea how much time had passed, and then we were halfway through our last song. It was as if everything happened beyond my control, and I didn't have to think about a thing I was doing. My fingers just moved to the right place at the right time. I didn't miss a beat of a single song, I timed hitting the pedals for distortion perfectly, and the songs that sounded good to us somehow translated to everyone in that hall. When I slid my first finger down to the fifth fret of my guitar, the last chord rang out and reverberated into the walls of the room. The crowd started applauding, turning excitedly to talk to each other, and some climbed up on stage to congratulate us. The applause felt amazing, but it wasn't what I remember best from that night.

As I looked around the room from my chair, I realised I didn't feel any different to anyone on the stage. I didn't see anyone staring or pointing at me and my differently shaped body, and I was suddenly aware that this was something I could do: I could take to the stage in front of friends and strangers, and if I played well, I could not only be accepted and appreciated, but regardless of the way I looked, I could move people with my skill and my musicianship. I could still set my own terms.

***

I'm writing about this over twenty years after it happened. I can still remember so much about that gig; the smell of the hall, scurrying up onto the stage with my crutches, and the feeling of being recognised for who I was, not what I looked like. We eventually did record a demo in a tiny music production studio nearby, and I keep that CD in a box full of special memories from my life. While the band fell apart before we reached college, and I stopped playing guitar as much (I still have an acoustic I noodle on occasionally), the experience of pushing myself to play in public was the momentum I needed to believe I could be a professional writer. A big part of my job is still taking to the stage in front of strangers and having the confidence to express myself, regardless of how I look. And that journey started with my guitar, three good friends and me seeing a chance, being terrified, but taking it anyway.

Why Do You Feel Sorry for Me?

by Ali Abbas

Iraq and United Kingdom

Ali Abbas, interviewed by James Catchpole

I grew up on a farm. We had a very big farm on the edge of Baghdad. We had lots of sheep, cows, goats, chickens, you know? I was a farmer. I loved my farm. We were farmers until the war started.

Before the war I was just 12. I was playing football – I was good at football. But my dream was to have a PlayStation. We weren't rich – you needed to be rich to buy a PlayStation and all the games. In Iraq we had sanctions. America put Iraq into sanctions for a long time – ten years before the war, maybe even more. So we couldn't get these things like PlayStations. I used to see them and wish I could have them. When we were young, we used to go to a special café – they had one PlayStation and you had to be in a queue to play. I used to queue for over an hour to have a game. We were playing a football game and there was also *Tekken*, you know, fighting.

Then I remember the Iraqi army preparing all the time, moving weapons. When it started, we knew. We knew we were under a state of war. We were very scared. I was young, and hearing all the planes flying, it was the scariest thing you can imagine, especially when you hear the bombs. I remember we were always hiding next to our mother, and she was telling us, 'No, you don't have to worry about it, it is very far away.' But we knew Baghdad was not safe – that most of the fighting would be in Baghdad – so we moved to my uncle's place in Hillah, one of the cities near Babylon. We moved there for over ten days. Then we decided now it looks quiet, we should go back to Baghdad, to our farm – we had cows, you know?

If we were one day later, this probably wouldn't have happened.

It was the day we came back, the 30th of March 2003 – that night. It was a bomb – an aeroplane strike.

How could it be an accident? We were farmers – we had our cows outside our homes. And you can see with the technology they have, they can see exactly what is there, you know? They were just dropping bombs indiscriminately.

Five houses got destroyed – maybe six – and sixteen people died in that attack: my parents and my brother, my uncle and my auntie and my cousins, and my neighbours. I had only stepsisters who survived, and my other uncle.

I was taken straight to hospital and my injuries were so bad. There was a journalist at the hospital, taking pictures. He said to the doctors, 'Take me to the worst case,' so they took him to me. I remember him taking pictures, but I was in so much pain. The first hospital I was in, everything was running out, so they had to move me. The second was the only working hospital in Baghdad. It was so crowded. I was in a room with maybe forty people. I started to have infections there, then the doctors said, 'If he stays here, he will die.'

The Americans flew me to a military medical camp. One of the doctors there, he was trying to treat me. He had a little TV, like a DVD player with a screen on it. He put this on and I was watching a cartoon on it. It was *Tom and Jerry*. They were taking care of the wounds, and I never said anything. There were so many things that I had never seen before.

It was the journalist, he helped me to get out of Iraq. He is Australian – I still have him on Facebook. He interviewed me and I said, 'Why did you help me?' He told me that it was a great story and he got paid so well. The pictures got so viral at that time, all over TV. And then after he was thinking, **how can I leave and not do anything about this young boy? I need to do something to help him.** And so he was speaking to Kuwait and he was speaking to Jordan and he was telling them, 'We need to help this boy.' I don't know how he organised it, but Kuwait decided to take me.

They moved me from Baghdad to Kuwait in a military plane – it was my first time on a plane. I just wanted the soldiers to show me the view from the window, to see what it was like, flying in the air. I think I was probably the first Iraqi to enter Kuwait at this time because the situation since Iraq invaded Kuwait, politically it was broken. My uncle was so concerned about how the Kuwaitis would receive us, but it was very good – Kuwaiti people were so helpful.

I met Ahmed in the hospital in Kuwait. I was in intensive care there. My uncle heard a little boy screaming and shouting and crying. He was from Iraq and he was injured too, and now he was in the room next door to me. We watched cartoons together. The doctors asked me, 'What do you need?' I said, 'I need exactly the cartoon I watched before.' So we watched *Tom and Jerry*.

Ahmed's parents were still alive and he was in a better situation than me. So I was more famous – I got more of the attention. He was absolutely fine with that. He didn't want to be the famous one. I was the famous one, but it wasn't for good reasons! I wasn't a singer or an actor or a football player. So Ahmed didn't mind at all. Ahmed is more than a brother to me. We have been through things together. We live in the same house, so he is still in the room next door to me, twenty years later!

***

My story at that moment was so powerful. So many people in Europe and around the world, they were against the war. So when they heard about my story and they saw my pictures, still in hospital with all those burns . . . In the streets in England, and in Europe, they had my picture at demonstrations.

When I was in Kuwait and I was in a bad situation in hospital, my uncle was telling me about all the messages I was receiving, and I was receiving maybe about forty or fifty cards a day. And I got so many gifts. So many gifts! One was a mobile phone. I received a bicycle – I couldn't drive it! And one of those gifts, it was a PlayStation.

A politician from England came to visit me in hospital
– she brought me the PlayStation. And I was struggling
with how to play, you know. I was thinking, **my dream,
it came at the wrong time**. I had a turn and I couldn't
play with it. At some point I was trying to play it with
my nose. But after that, I started working out how I can
play it with my feet. I had to learn to do everything with
my feet – to feed myself – but the PlayStation was the
most important. Feeding myself at that time, of course
someone else would come and do it. But PlayStation, I
learned quickly.

Everyone was so surprised that I was so quick at
adapting to using my feet, because I just lost my
arms like four months before. I am so good at playing
PlayStation with my feet now, if I wake up tomorrow and
I have arms, I will still play PlayStation with my feet.

When I was still injured, I didn't accept anything
from Americans. As a twelve-year-old in Baghdad, I
knew America was leading the invasion of Iraq. All that
was mentioned was America, America, you know? I
hated everything that I received from Americans. I had
so much anger at that time.

But, you know, things got cooled off. I met Americans, I
met British people – most of them were against the war,

and they were so touched, they were in tears when they saw me. They showed me so much kindness.

I made so many friends, you know. A Man United fan, he was sending me so many signed shirts and footballs from Manchester United, you know, David Beckham – this is how I became a Manchester United fan.

I made a friend, she came to Kuwait because she saw my picture. She's from France. When she saw me on TV she just said, 'I want to go and meet Ali.' She left her work and she came and she stayed in Kuwait for maybe four months while I was in hospital, just to be next to me. I don't know why – I never asked her, you know. But she is an amazing woman – she gave me advice and has been always there at my side since 2003. She later became my godmother. I still speak to her every day.

I had offers to come to America, and they were very good offers and I could have gone there, but I never wanted to go to America. I had an offer to go to Canada and I wanted to go to Canada, but they said, 'We will take you, but we will not take Ahmed.' So I said, 'I will not travel without Ahmed.' I also had an offer from England, so I said, 'I will only come if Ahmed comes,' and they accepted that.

A headmaster, when he saw what happened to me and Ahmed, he offered us a free place in his private school in Wimbledon. It was a very nice school. The headmaster was very good. The teachers – everyone – was so supportive.

When we came to England, we came on a private jet to a military airport – it was the Sheikh of Kuwait – he sent us on one of his private jets. We arrived in England late 2003. And when we first came to London, my godmother was always there, and my friend, the Man United fan, organised a trip for us to go and visit Manchester United and meet all the players: Ryan Giggs, Paul Scholes, Roy Keane, Cristiano Ronaldo. I still have the pictures.

Some charities used to take me to events to speak about my experiences. At that time I was still young, and they were pushing me to go on and speak and these kind of things, when I first came here. At that time I didn't know if I could do it, and they were saying, 'You **have** to come, you **have** to do this.'

These things happen in charities. Later I stopped having any involvement with charities.

But I hope that maybe in the future I'll make my own

charity. I was lucky, you know – I was one of the lucky ones. If this journalist hadn't come to that hospital and taken that picture of me, then I wouldn't be alive. I got the opportunity. There are so many people who don't have an opportunity. Here in Baghdad I see so many people who have lost limbs, who are disabled and couldn't afford to do anything. I want to help with whatever I can. From my own money sometimes, I do try to help some people. One time I got a wheelchair to a disabled boy, which made him so happy.

Life will always move on. For a long time I was angry inside, and sad, depressed. For a long time. That made me hate being alive. But after that I decided being angry and depressed, it will not help. And I should just enjoy life and forget about anything that happened to me and move forward.

One day I decided to buy a car, and I said, 'I'll drive this.' I didn't know how to drive it but I just wanted to drive it, and I found a way to use one of my feet on the accelerator and the brake, and the other one on the steering wheel. I didn't adapt anything in the car. I just worked it out myself. My legs are very flexible.

Here in Iraq, when you put your foot into someone's face it is an insult. Here, we have so many checkpoints, and when I am arriving, the policemen, they see my foot pointing in their direction, and they are shouting at me, 'When you come here to a checkpoint, you have to show some respect!' But after they find out it's the only way I can drive they are so ashamed!

My son is six. He is good with this kind of thing. He is so OK with being around disabled people. If he sees a guy who is missing a limb, he doesn't even look – he thinks it's normal. My son comes to stay at my family's house in Baghdad – we have a new house, about 600 metres from where it all happened.

I never want anyone to feel sorry for me, so anyone who starts to get a bit emotional, I say, 'Why? Why do you feel sorry for me? I don't feel sorry for myself.' There's no reason for someone to feel sorry.

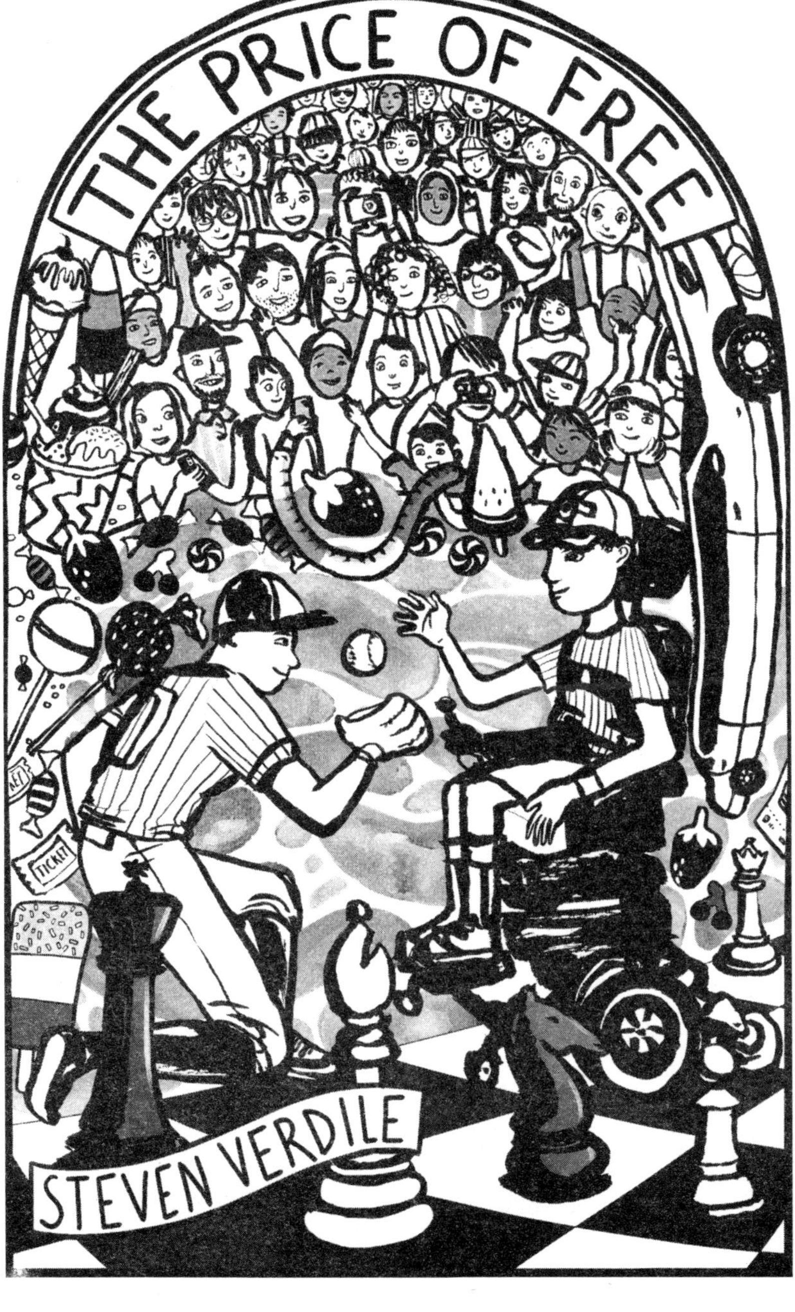
THE PRICE OF FREE
STEVEN VERDILE

The Price of Free

by Steven Verdile

United States

The Stuff

I love stuff. T-shirts and sneakers, stickers and pins, tickets for events, or even just a small piece of candy. I've always loved stuff, and who can blame me? I bet you love stuff, too.

When I was a kid, I got a lot of stuff for free. Some of it was little, like a free SpongeBob ice pop from the ice-cream truck, and some of it was big, like a brand-new computer with fancy software.

For my first few years of receiving stuff, I didn't even really realise it was free, or that stuff normally costs money, or that I was receiving it specifically because I was disabled. I had no concept of money back then. Sometimes I wish I still didn't.

The Mouse

In November of 2000, just a few days before my fourth birthday, I received what can only be described as the ultimate offering of free stuff. The Make-A-Wish Foundation sent me, a little wheelchair-using kid with spinal muscular atrophy, and my family on an all-expenses-paid vacation to the house of the mouse, the kingdom of magic, Orlando Florida's Walt Disney World.

Make-A-Wish sent a limo to our house to bring us to the train station, and reserved us a beautiful cottage in their very own Give Kids the World Village. At Give Kids the World, every child was treated like royalty, ice cream was always free and the mayor was a man in a rabbit costume. At the end of their trip, each lucky child decorated the ceiling of the resort lobby with their name on a small gold star.

One day during the vacation, we celebrated my fourth birthday at the Mickey Mouse breakfast buffet. With a mouse-shaped chocolate chip waffle on my dish and a chocolate-stained grin on my face, I was having an absolutely amazing day . . . until suddenly I wasn't.

A group of waiters had walked out with a cupcake and candles, and started to sing 'Happy Birthday' to me. I tensed up, and as they got closer, guests in the restaurant started to join in. Dozens of families stared at me, the little birthday wheelchair boy, as they sang along in celebration and waved their green napkins in the air. I started to cry, and my mom picked me up from my chair to hold me. I don't know if Mickey's restaurant guests always cheer so passionately for children's birthdays. Maybe they do. But I wouldn't be surprised if my wheelchair gave them a little extra excitement.

Either way, for a four-year-old me, it was too much. Too much attention, too overwhelming, too many people. I cried more. I wanted to go back to being the inconspicuous kid eating breakfast with his family. At that moment I would've surely traded fancy Disney waffles for the frozen plain ones in our house.

The Price

Getting to go on a once-in-a-lifetime vacation is an incredible experience, and I certainly wouldn't take it back, but there was a deeper reason why the attention at a seemingly normal Chef Mickey's birthday breakfast didn't feel good. Though I didn't understand fully as a four-year-old, maybe I had a slight sense that there was a price to that trip, even though it was 'free'.

I learned later that Make-A-Wish doesn't grant these amazing opportunities to every child. They grant them to sick and disabled children, and sometimes to children who have a chance of dying young. I didn't ever think

I was a dying kid, especially because my parents never spoke like that. I always believed I would live a normal, long life, and I'm twenty-seven years old now, as healthy as I have ever been.

This meant that the people at Make-A-Wish, and maybe the people at Mickey's breakfast, saw me with a bit of pity. That's why the attention felt bad. They thought that just because I was disabled that my life was sad, and they wanted to make it a little better, even if it was just for a few days or minutes. That is what those special vacations are for.

Once I was old enough to realise this, I had questions. If I **wasn't** sad or dying, did I still deserve Disney? Did I steal that trip from some other sicker or sadder kid? Or is being 'just' disabled enough to warrant a VIP pass to the happiest place on earth?

There are no real answers to these questions, and I know now that's not how charities work. The way they really work is that they have a lot of money, and they try to pick people who need it most, but really they're just guessing. Their intentions are to make people happier, and hey, a fun trip to Disney will work on most people.

Still, the older I got, the more I started thinking about the price of that free stuff, and if I deserve the stuff, and if it's wrong to accept it.

The Candyman

The Make-A-Wish Foundation offered some really fabulous free stuff, but when you are a clearly, visibly disabled child who uses a wheelchair that weighs five times your own weight, the same sentiment could be found in everyday life too. One time a man in a convenience store tried to slip me a $20 bill, and told me to buy as much candy as I wanted. My mom refused it, gave him back the money, and bought me a more reasonable, smaller amount of candy.

What made this offer different from the Make-A-Wish trip? And why did my mom accept one, but not the other? Even at that young age I knew both offers had similar intentions. Perhaps the difference was that my family could afford to buy some candy, but couldn't so easily splurge on an accessible and luxurious resort vacation to Disney with all of the bells and whistles. Or perhaps the difference was that the trip was paid for by a wealthy foundation, not just a well-meaning dude in a shop. Either way, I learned that sometimes you accept offers like that, and sometimes you don't.

The Choice

Just a few years went by, and suddenly I was the one,
not my parents, deciding when to accept free stuff and
when to decline. At times, the offers made me feel like
all the bits of the real me were bundled into one generic
'disabled kid' label. 'Disabled kids' like me were sad and
unlucky, and kind adults gave them things to make up
for that. In return, we should be abundantly grateful and
remind them that they did a good thing by enhancing
the quality of our lives – lives less fortunate than theirs. I
didn't like that dynamic, but I did like stuff, and it made
those decisions difficult.

By the time I was eleven or twelve, the times that I did
accept such offers felt routine and transactional. Like
a choreographed dance, I knew exactly when to say
thank you, when to ask to skip the line and when to act
surprised by the extra lollipop I would be given by the
cashier. It didn't feel like a scam, because I couldn't even
avoid it if I tried.

Often I played along, not because I actually wanted the
special treatment, but because I didn't want to seem

ungrateful. I convinced myself that I wanted to please the adults, and that it made me feel good to make them feel good. I see now that my logic was pretty backwards there, but at least this way I felt like I was in charge, and that I was the generous one. I was doing a kind favour by sharing fake, or sometimes real, joy and gratitude.

Still, every time I faced these decisions, I felt conflicted.

The Telethon

Each year, I experienced that feeling during the famous Muscular Dystrophy Association telethons, hosted by Jerry Lewis. The organisation would host a twenty-four-hour television special to raise money for a cure, and would show video after video of cute children with muscular dystrophy. Most years I would watch from home, but a few times I attended the event in person, and was once featured in it as an MDA summer camp kid, swimming in the pool and having a great time thanks to the 'generous donations from viewers at home'.

The last time I attended, I saw The Village People, an American disco group who famously dressed in various occupation-based costumes, performing their song 'Y.M.C.A.' (obviously). The dance involves mostly upper-arm movement, and was surprisingly achievable by many of the wheelchair kiddos in the audience.

I did genuinely feel grateful that MDA had these fundraisers because the MDA summer camp was a blast, and research for treatment seemed like a good thing. Still, it felt a little icky seeing myself and so many of my friends paraded around as mascots for a charity. The message was never, 'All kids deserve nice lives so let's make sure these kids have nice lives too.' It was always, 'These sick children have sad lives so let's give them a little treat, and maybe we can find a cure so no more kids will be like them.' When you're ten years old, that's a lot to take in. It made me uncomfortable, and no amount of dancing construction workers or police officers could distract from that.

The Internet

As I got older and busier, my participation in the telethon and other disability events dwindled. I don't regret those experiences, but it felt nice to no longer make them a priority, and by the time I was in high school, I pretty much stopped attending them completely. Instead, I focused my energy on the things that were fun for me, like travelling to baseball stadiums and playing in competitive chess tournaments.

Chess felt like the opposite of those telethons and fundraisers. At every match there was a loser, and no amount of pity or inspiration could prevent that inevitable outcome. Losing was fun because I knew I earned that loss fair and square. And winning was even better, because I knew when I won I wasn't viewed as inspirational or tragic – I was viewed as smart, and my peers respected that. That is unless . . . Did I ever receive a pity-win? I certainly hope not.

I really started to enjoy spending time on the internet then too, for the same reason. Sometimes I even combined the two, and played chess on the internet where pity-wins could never be an issue. On message boards nobody knew I was disabled, and I could happily chit-chat or talk sports or make jokes without my disability being a factor. When my post made it to the front page of Reddit with 100,000 upvotes, it wasn't because people pitied me, it was because I was a nerd with a good meme. The internet, like chess, felt fair, and it felt like any achievement or attention there was earned, not gifted.

The Acceptance

As I approached adulthood, I spent as much time as I

could in places that felt fair in that way. Still, I would occasionally find myself facing opportunities for free stuff that wasn't so free. I was mastering the fine balance of learning when to perform the ritual, and when to decline the offer.

After years and years of these situations, I ultimately learned to accept these opportunities not to please adults, or to avoid offending them, but only for myself. I told myself that my life was in fact hard in some ways. I had to deal with inaccessibility and discrimination and people constantly underestimating me. If my friends could go rock-climbing and waterskiing, and could visit each other's stair-filled houses with ease, it was only fair that I got moved to the front row at the Disney Channel concert. And looking back, I know now that it didn't even matter if the stuff was 'earned', what mattered was if it made me happy or if it made me feel bad.

A dollar bill or food from strangers became a hard pass, but getting to skip the line at a crowded event? How could you turn that down! I would only be playing myself by turning down the chance to see Aly & AJ up close.

The Pitch

In 2013, at the age of sixteen, I found myself in a situation not too different from that scary fourth birthday buffet. This time, instead of dozens of eyes on me, it was tens of thousands, and instead of being in Disney World, I was on the grass of Citi Field, the stadium of my favourite baseball team, the New York Mets. Most importantly, by now I had more confidence in my identity and a life full of experiences to lean on.

A friend of a friend of a friend, Sue, worked for the Mets for many years, and had become a friend of my family after we met at a game the year before. We talked a lot about the team, but also about how I started a small online business designing custom baseball cards for people, and how I had just enrolled at St John's University, her alma mater, with a full scholarship. She knew I was not only a huge Mets fan, but a hard-working teenager who was doing the best he could in a complicated life.

She invited me to come to the stadium early one day during batting practice, and I got to meet some of my favourite players. Just as batting practice was coming to an end, Sue approached me with the opportunity of a lifetime.

Every baseball game begins with a ceremonial 'first pitch', a tradition that I had watched in person probably a hundred times. Usually it is thrown by a longtime season ticket holder, or a celebrity, or a military veteran, but by some combination of goodwill, luck and generosity, that day it could be me.

When asked if I wanted to do it, I had to consider the cost of free. Was I ready to go in front of thirty thousand people and be the inspirational wheelchair teen? If they clap for me, are those pity claps? Everybody clapped when Rihanna threw out the first pitch, but I don't think they pitied her? Am I like, wheelchair Rihanna? I bet Rihanna would've gotten even more claps if she used a wheelchair.

I also thought about the physical act of throwing the ball. I had barely enough muscle in my arm to lift a baseball, let alone throw one. My best-case scenario was that I could throw it a few inches past my own feet. Would my wimpy throw be funny? Would it inspire people? It is a symbolic pitch after all, it doesn't really matter if it's a good throw . . . right?

All of these thoughts raced through my brain in just a few seconds. I had faced these decisions many times before, but never for anything so big. Ultimately I decided I wanted to do it. Not for the thousands of fans who would see it, or for Sue, who had generously arranged the opportunity, or for my family, who would surely be filming it on their phones. I wanted to do it for myself.

I loved the Mets. Why would I let the feelings of others stop me from doing something that, to me, is super-cool? And with that confidence, I accepted the opportunity.

Just minutes before the game began, I came out from inside the stadium tunnels and onto the field. The baseball in my bony hand felt like it weighed a hundred pounds, and I carefully positioned myself on the first-base line (the actual pitching mound is notoriously mound-shaped and inaccessible for wheelchairs). The stadium announcer said my name, and something about my disability, and thousands of Mets fans watched me prepare to start off a day of baseball.

I took a deep breath, reached back, and threw the baseball as hard as I possibly could. It barely left my hand. Fortunately my favourite baseball player, seven-time All-Star David Wright, was there to save me from embarrassment, and swiftly caught the ball before it could fall to my own feet.

People cheered, and looked at me, and it felt like my fourth birthday all over again. But this time I didn't cry. This time I couldn't help but smile, and I took the baseball with me to my seat. My family and I cheered on the Mets, and we watched them go on to win the game in dramatic comeback fashion. It was a fantastic day, and absolutely worth the price, even if it wasn't totally free.

MY OWN
WORDS FOR
MY OWN WORLD

SNOWMAN

POLLY ATKIN

My Own Words for My Own World

by Polly Atkin

United Kingdom

I still dream sometimes of the second school I went
to, the one where I spent most of my school days. I
dream myself back there, lost in the maze of its endless
staircases, its nonsense corridors. In my dreams it
grows and shrinks. The stairs become wobbly ladders,
rooms fold into rooms. I search for classrooms and find
cupboards. I search for toilets and find more stairs.
There is no map or guide to it, but there wasn't one in
real life either.

This school was a patchwork of big old houses linked
by a wide single-storied highway with squeaky lino on
the floor. A hundred years before we had our lessons
in them, our classrooms were living rooms, bedrooms,
drawings rooms and kitchens for Victorian families –
families with servants who needed secret staircases to
scurry up and down, so each block had two sets of stairs:
a wide one with banisters so tempting to slide down they
had brass knots screwed into them to stop you, and a
narrow one, squeezed into an awkward shape, hidden

behind everything. I remember a small room on the curve of those stairs. The school nurse sat in that room, and it was called the halfway house, as though the stairs were a mountain we had to climb. Our locker rooms were basements dug into the sandstone beneath, where metal grates blocked off tunnels that disappeared into the guts of the city. We called these the dungeons. The cool breath of ghosts sighed out of the dark mouth of those barred-off tunnels and I was scared to walk past them in case I got dragged down. In my dreams and my memories, the corridors and stairs are constantly moving with people, children and teachers, like busy roads. Impossible to cross from one side to the other without being knocked over. There was never enough time to get from one block to another, not when you couldn't run or scurry or throw yourself into the bubbling stream of other bodies, as I couldn't.

I joined this school when I was seven. We would start each day with an assembly in a small hall, which was also our gym, with its ropes and wooden bars along the walls to remind us of the pain and humiliation to come during PE lessons. We sat on the wooden floor, cross-legged, and stood for hymns. Sometimes someone fainted or got a nosebleed. No one was allowed to fidget or talk. There was no room for bodies that didn't do what was expected of them.

My body did not do what anyone expected, but no one knew why, not until I was grown up. I started primary school with a broken leg – this was the second time I'd broken my leg – and I spent part of the last year of junior school with one leg in plaster, too. I started senior school thinking I was fine, then I dislocated my knee for the first time before Christmas. I spent most of that year inching my way around on crutches, terrified of being shoved over on the stairs. As well as that, I had allergies. I was often ill and did not get better. When my skin broke, it did not heal. I was very tired all of the time. I struggled to eat and to sleep. Sometimes I could not make my body move. I had tonsilitis on and off for months. No one could tell me why this was, or whether these things were connected: why I fell over a lot, why I broke bones when I did, why I took so long to get over things. It was just the way I was.

Much later, I would find out it is because I was born with Ehlers-Danlos syndrome, or EDS. EDS is caused by a difference in the way my body makes an ingredient in my bones, skin and muscles, a protein called collagen, which is a substance you can find in every part of every person's body. The difference I have makes my collagen more stretchy and fragile, less elastic. For people with EDS, our bones and our skin and our organs and our blood vessels are all more fragile, and our joints slip in and out of place because our ligaments and muscles can't hold them tightly. As well as our joints, it can affect the way our blood moves around our bodies, the way food moves through our stomachs and our guts. It can make it difficult to stand up, difficult to sleep, and it makes us very tired. It can affect the way we process pain, and also create a lot of pain, as even little things can cause us injuries. It can make us more prone to illness, and slower to heal. It can be part of a cluster of linked conditions, including autism, which could explain so much about how I experience the world – why it seems like such a hard surface to keep falling onto and into.

But when I was at school I did not know this. EDS is considered to be an invisible disability, but my difference was not invisible, it was just not understood. I was told I was too sensitive. That I was lazy or difficult. That I was always making a fuss about nothing. At my first school, I cried a lot and refused to eat lunch because the textures were all wrong and I couldn't swallow it, so I went hungry every day. At my second school, I learned not to cry because even my friends laughed at me when I did. I learned to hold my pain in, no matter how much it hurt. And everything hurt. Things that didn't hurt other people hurt me: pinches or nudges, knocks in the playground or in sport. I got tired out by things that didn't tire out other people. I told my mum that getting through each day felt like trying to run through treacle. By the time I was nine, my knees hurt so much that we went back to the hospital, looking for answers, but they weren't very helpful. Back when I was four, they had said I had to do dance lessons to help my joints. This time they said I had to stop the dance lessons to help my joints. It didn't make sense to me. I was in pain, I was tired, everything was difficult. They made me feel like it was difficult because I was difficult.

***

This wasn't the only way I knew I was different.

When I started my first school, I didn't just have a broken leg to mark me out, I also had a language all of my own, one that nobody else could speak or understand. Not even my own family fully understood what I was saying, though they had got used to making good guesses. I had been speaking my own language, and that language alone, since I'd started talking as a baby. I had a lot to say, but none of it in English. At first, my mum and dad thought I would grow out of it. But I didn't. I carried on, as stubborn as I still am, clinging to my own words. I don't know why I did it, I don't know why or how it started. I understood everything other people said and I had plenty to say back, just in my own way.

My mum took me to a doctor who treated speech differences. They said my language did not follow any patterns, and they could not tell what I was doing or why, but they said I needed therapy to make me speak English. The only problem was the waiting list was long, which meant I started school still confidently speaking a language my teachers heard as just noise. I don't remember it being a particular problem. I made friends. I did lessons. I don't remember feeling like no one could understand me, but I do remember having problems with teachers. It did not occur to me at the time it was because they couldn't understand anything I was telling them.

My form teacher Mrs F – the only one at that school I loved – admitted to my mum she couldn't understand a word I was saying. She told Mum she'd have to take it on trust I was reading what was on a page, because she couldn't tell. I don't think I knew, as I read aloud confidently, enjoying the story of *Peter the Blue Pirate*, that the sounds I was making were not the same sounds other children made. I was always getting in trouble at that school. Sometimes for things I did or didn't do, sometimes for things other people did. In my first year, I was accused every lunchtime of throwing my potatoes on the floor to hide them, but it was the girl who sat next to me who did that. Every day I proclaimed my innocence to the teacher, as though before a judge, and was found guilty. The other girl's granny had told her that if she didn't like the food, she should throw it under the table. She was just following orders, but it was me who got in trouble – every day losing playtime to mop up someone else's lunch. I wonder now if I was not believed because they simply didn't know what I was saying.

We were still waiting for a speech therapist appointment, but the wait went on and on. Mum found out that Mrs C, the mother of a girl I played with at playgroup, was a speech therapist, and begged her to take us on as a private case.

I loved Mrs C but I resented her rules and her demands. She would hide picture cards around a room and, when I found them, I had to tell her the 'right' word for the picture on them, and by 'right' word, she meant her word, the word other people used, not my word. I don't remember much of these lessons, but I remember the moment I caved, gave in, handed over my language. I had found a snowman card. I wanted the lesson to be over so badly, so I could be free to play. I remember saying my word for snowman over and over, and being asked again and again, 'What is the right word?' I remember that I knew it, **snowman**, but I didn't want to give it. It was **a** word, alright, but not **the** word. I remember my frustration and my anger. I remember sunlight through a window. I remember realising my only way out was to surrender. So, I did. I was disappointed in myself, cross and frustrated with everyone else. I felt like I'd cheated myself, or given up an important secret.

I don't remember any of my own language now, though for years I would wake up with the feeling I had been dreaming in words that weren't English, and knew it was still there inside me, sleeping. I wonder where it is now. I wonder if sometimes when I am grasping for a word I can't remember, it's because somewhere deep and forgotten in me it is being translated, without me thinking.

***

So, I was used to being different at school – moving differently, speaking differently. Because no one knew why, no one knew how to help, and that was the worst thing. Some people tried to be understanding. In my last year of junior school I was one of several children who couldn't run in the school sports day, but the teachers still wanted us to take part, so they made up a game just for us. We sat in chairs on the field and threw hoops at cones.

It was meant to be fun and inclusive, but throwing hoops was just as hard for me as running and I was really bad at it. It was humiliating. It singled us out, the four of us with our special game, as different. It made us into something to stare at. I would rather have not taken part at all, but that was not an option.

When I dislocated my knee in the first year of senior school, I had just bought a hockey stick I would never get to use. I was told I couldn't do contact sports anymore, and apart from swimming, all of our school games were contact sports.

Because there was an idea that I would get better, for the whole of that year I was made to sit on the sidelines and watch every sports lesson, so that I would understand it when I was allowed to join in again.

I was not the only one. There was J, who sometimes could not join in with games lessons with her prosthetic legs. There was F, who'd had an operation on one leg which meant she couldn't walk on it and had left her with chronic pain. There was H and E with different back problems. As the years went on, our numbers grew. Soon there were four or five of us on the regular.

It seemed like a kind of punishment to make us sit in the cold and watch everyone else run around. We could feel the eyes of them on us as they moved so easily. We were highlighted in neon, bright as our pain.

Eventually, we managed to get the teachers to let us spend sports lessons in the library instead. We became a non-sports club, a beanbag gang, meeting and chatting in low voices between the shelves. The library became our sanctuary.

We were together in our apartness. A library club no librarian chose. Most of us didn't know why our bodies did or didn't do the things they did, but we could share our pain together. We didn't have to pretend around each other. It was my first experience – my only experience back then – of disabled kinship, though we would not have used those words. We had no role models to help us understand ourselves and each other, but we had the library. We had that quiet space between the shelves, and we had books.

When I think of a time at school when I felt relaxed, safe, it is on those beanbags, between the shelves, hidden from the librarian's view, and in the company of others who lived with pain.

***

I'm not going to lie to you. School was hard and sad, and I would not go back there. But I survived. I learned things from it and not all of them were bad. Most importantly, in the years since, I have learned that the things that made school hard for me are also the things that make grown-up life rich and wonderful for me. I gave up a language but now I'm an author and I make my own world, from my own words, in the best way I can. I am sensitive, I notice things other people don't, I see things in a different way, I feel things deeply. At school these can be dangerous things, but they are also what make me a good writer, a good artist. I hope they make me a thoughtful, caring person, though I know there have been times they have made me feel scared and alone, and because of that, they have made me unkind and impatient with others.

Now I know myself better, I am not scared, and I know I am in excellent company. I hope for a world where people like me – people like us – can experience the good parts without the bad, without feeling alone or judged. I think we could make it together, don't you?

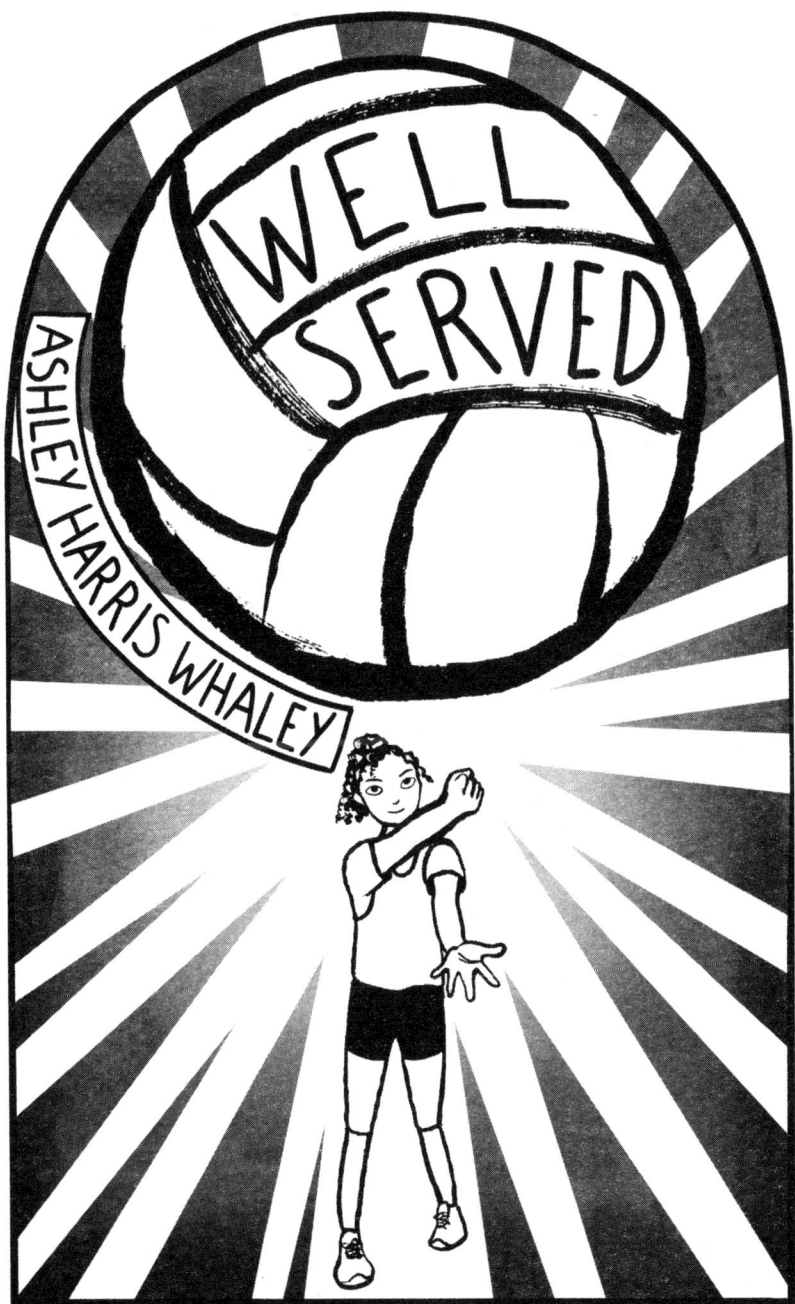

Well Served

by Ashley Harris Whaley

United States

Let's start our tale on a Thursday evening in May 2007. I was standing on stage in a stuffy room with walls festooned with floor-to-ceiling orange carpet. The room was my high school's auditorium, and I was about to receive an award for sportsmanship and perseverance. Now, you might be thinking, **why were the walls covered in orange carpet?** or **oh of course the disabled kid is getting the team award for sportsmanship and perseverance**. Either way, I don't blame you. The second point does seem like a cliché, I know. And on one level, I reckon it probably is. But there was a little more to it than that – for me, anyway.

Maybe I'll rewind a bit to see how we got here. Seems like that might help.

Back in the fall of 2003, I was eleven and entering sixth grade. Here in the States, that marks the beginning of our middle school years. Middle school usually brings about new freedoms, and lots of changes. One thing that hadn't changed for me was the expectation that I was to stretch at least once per day while at school. Stretch, you say? Well, my parents and teachers thought it would be important for me to keep my stiff leg muscles as limber as possible while sitting at a desk all day, because I have CP.

What's CP, you ask?

OK, let's travel **all** the way back in time to 1992, shall we? (I promise we'll come back again!)

In July of that year, my mom was about six months pregnant, and my parents were on a beach vacation with their best friends to celebrate the 4th of July. They thought it would be nothing but a routine weekend at the beach, and spoiler alert: it was not. Without boring you with all the details, my mom's unfortunate uterus decided it would be best to have me out of there a full three months early. In all of the hullabaloo of being born, my brain was deprived of oxygen. My lifelong souvenir from this vacation to the beach? Cerebral palsy (or CP for short), which, for the uninitiated, means that someone has trouble controlling their muscles and moving about. It looks different for everyone, but for me, it means that my core muscles are really weak and the muscles in my legs and feet are very tight. My walk is an interesting one, to put it lightly. Let's just say that no one ever fails to notice it.

So anyway, my parents went from their beach vacation to an intensive care unit for babies. They stayed there with me for the first three months of my life, far from home.

Well, I may have been born in a beach town, but I come from a small community in the wilds of the southern Appalachian Mountains. It's a close-knit community with generations of roots. My classmates' parents all went to school with my parents in the 1980s, and my classmates' grandparents all went to school with my grandparents in the late 1950s. It seems cliché to say that everyone knew everyone, but we really, really did. I could look up into the bleachers and see my papaw sitting beside my best friend Cassie's Granddaddy Gerald, two men bonding over girls' volleyball just like they had bonded in army basic training together in 1960.

But what do two old mountain men watching their granddaughters play volleyball have to do with all of this? Why does that matter? It matters because it's hard to explain how fully **known** I was within my school and community. And for this disabled kid? That mattered quite a bit.

So, when I ended up being born very ahead of schedule, at an inopportune place and time, my community knew all about it. Friends came to visit, and back home folks started hosting benefits and raising funds. A few years later, everyone rallied around replacing the playground at our elementary school with a new one that I could access. Everyone knew about my disability, but a lot (or maybe even most) of my peers didn't even know what it was called. I was just Ashley and that was just the way I happened to be.

Eleven years later, I'm starting middle school, and we're back in 2003. (Told you we'd come back again!)

Our school was so tiny that the middle and high schools both shared the same building, which meant we middle schoolers all knew who the high schoolers were. As luck would have it, the person assigned to be my stretching partner was the senior captain of the volleyball team. She was so pretty and fun, and I couldn't believe my luck that we would get to hang out together each day.

By the end of day one I had decided that I had to be just like her. Or at least, a lot like her. And what was the first step in that plan? Learning to play volleyball. That was an interesting choice for me, honestly.

I'll let y'all in on a little secret: I was a pretty high-strung pre-teen. One who evolved into a very high-strung teenager (and then into an adult who thankfully learned how to mellow out just a tad). I felt a crushing pressure to be 'the best', and as much as I hate to admit it now, to prove myself. Since I've had some years to look back on it all, I know the reason. It all came from being disabled, and some of it was self-imposed, sure. But there's a pressure from society at play here, too. One that says you're a whole lot more palatable to the world if you excel, and if you prove yourself.

So, I found places where I could be the best in ways that came very naturally to me: straight As, class president in each grade, debate team, drama club, you name it. Now, volleyball wasn't a place where I was going to excel. In fact, there was no chance I was ever going to be the best. So why, exactly, did I sign myself up?

For one thing, it was just the thing to do. In a school as small as mine, almost all my friends played, too. And that meant hanging out on long bus rides over the mountain to schools in other counties for our away games. And then there was bench-sitting, which meant engaging in one of my favourite pastimes: commentary. If I'm one thing, it's chatty. At any given moment, there might have been five of us girls sitting on the bench, and having a dang good time doing so.

But despite a newfound love for sports commentary, there was still a game to play. An actual competitive sport! And here's the thing that surprised me: even though I was never going to be the best at it, I actually **loved** playing volleyball.

You might think that CP plus volleyball would equal some kind of recipe for disaster. And you wouldn't be completely wrong. What people usually misunderstand about CP is that the issue isn't really with the muscles and the tendons. The issue is with the brain, which controls all of these things! So, my reaction times are slower than slow. Volleyball needs you to be quicker than quick. My muscles needed my brain to always think three steps ahead in order to not miss any passes, digs or sets. And since my brain couldn't quite manage that, quite a few balls were missed!

But my coaches quickly figured out that you don't need nearly as much co-ordination or as quick reflexes to serve the ball as you need to make other moves in the sport. So there it was: I could serve. My teammates could serve, too, and most of them had impressive overhand serves with jumps, ball spins or both. I couldn't do any of that. But it didn't matter at all, because you know what I could do? Serve underhand like an old-school volleyball grandma. And the best part was, I pretty reliably managed to get the ball over the net. Sometimes we needed a serve that might not score any points by itself, but probably wouldn't lose us any either – and then I was the girl for the job.

If you are disabled, your growing-up years can be littered with half-hearted attempts at inclusion that are done for no other reason than to check a box. You can be made to feel like an exception or a big deal, or that you ought to be grateful that you're being included, as if that's the be-all and end-all. As if the whole point of inclusion is that everyone else walks away feeling better about themselves.

Most of us have been there at one time or another, and it never feels good. The beautiful thing about volleyball, though, is that it felt different to me. I didn't feel like anyone was including me on the team just because I was disabled. I didn't feel like anyone pitied me or felt obligated to have me there. As far as I was concerned, I was on the team because I loved spending time with my friends, and because I found that I loved playing the game.

So I gleefully sat on the bench, knowing it was unlikely that I'd have much playing time. I would sub in, serve, and sub right back out. Since my underhand vaulted the ball into the air much higher than an overhand would, I had yet to score any points from serves. But it wasn't about that, for me. It was pure fun with absolutely no expectations, and sometimes I think that might be the best kind.

And that's how it went right up into high school where, in October of ninth grade, when I was fourteen, two pretty major things happened.

First, an actual miracle. We were playing the worst team in our league. I subbed in to serve once we had a pretty sizeable lead. And then, something extraordinary happened. My granny serve **actually** scored points. Yes, you read that right! The 's' on points was not a typo. Three serves, three points in a row. The crowd went wild. My teammates literally lifted me off the ground. Parents of the other players began clapping, while their daughters stood on the other side of the net, staring up into the bleachers with absolute bewilderment.

Looking back, I'm sure this must have been a spectacle. The parents of the other players didn't know me at all. Maybe they just assumed that I was a poor little disabled girl, given a pity position on her team, who had somehow managed to score a few points. But even so, they were clapping right alongside all of our folks who had made the trip over the mountain for the game: moms, dads, grandmas and granddads who knew that I had actually worked really hard to learn those serves; that I had trained and conditioned at all the same workouts and practices as my teammates, coaching my body to its maximum potential. Which was no small feat. So maybe it was a spectacle. Even if it was, I didn't even mind, because I **had** earned this.

Now for the second (and far less exciting) event of that October. I found out that I would be having major surgery the following summer to realign bones in both legs, and it ended up being scheduled for the day after my fifteenth birthday. What luck!

I didn't exactly spell it straight out for everyone, but my coach and I both knew that this was likely the end of the road for me. We knew that I would be physically unable to play in the tenth grade and maybe even the eleventh, because I would be relearning to walk and rehabbing for at least a year. The two of us sat down to have a conversation about what would likely happen after that. I remember her saying, 'Ashley, I love having you on the team. As you advance to the varsity level you probably won't be seeing much playing time anymore and the practices and skill mastery will be a lot harder for you, but if you're OK with that then I would still love to have you.'

I thought long and hard about it. Mostly, I thought about my insatiable need to be the very best at everything I do. To leave no room for doubt that I'm capable and that I deserve to be taken seriously. Would giving up volleyball feel like quitting? Maybe like failure? Or even worse, like giving up on myself?

Before playing volleyball, I had rarely (if ever?) given myself permission not to excel. Or to be free from the endless cycle of proving something to the world while also proving something to myself. Honestly, I'm not sure I realised this at the time but volleyball freed me from those expectations. I was never going to be the best at it, competing against my non-disabled peers. But it allowed me a different opportunity: to stop measuring myself against impossible standards.

All of that, ultimately, made it very difficult to give up.

It wasn't a decision that I **had** to make, but what I **did** have to do was take a really long detour that was out of my control. By the time our twelfth-grade season rolled around, I would have been two years out of practice and out of shape, and preoccupied with other things like scholarship applications, senior plays, student government, college visits and all that. A hard truth is that sometimes even the things you love aren't the right fit for you anymore. Life goes on.

So, this brings us back to the spring of 2007 (and our last trip in the time machine). There I was, up on stage in the room with the orange-carpeted walls, getting an award for sportsmanship and perseverance. And who came back to town for the evening to present me with the award? None other than the former senior captain and my sixth-grade stretching partner. I do love a full-circle moment!

Volleyball gave me many things. It gave me great times with great friends, sleepovers and camaraderie. It gave me stronger muscles, sharper reflexes, more energy and less pain. It gave me a chance to be truly and fully included for exactly who I am and exactly what I could do.

But now, quite a few years on down the road, I can see something else it gave me. Something just as important – or perhaps even more so. Volleyball gave me freedom.

It freed me from the constant urge to prove myself. It freed me from the crushing weight of always having to be the best in the hopes that the rest of the world might see my value. It gave me time to do something for the pure joy of it. And it gave me the chance to see my own value without demanding that others see it, too.

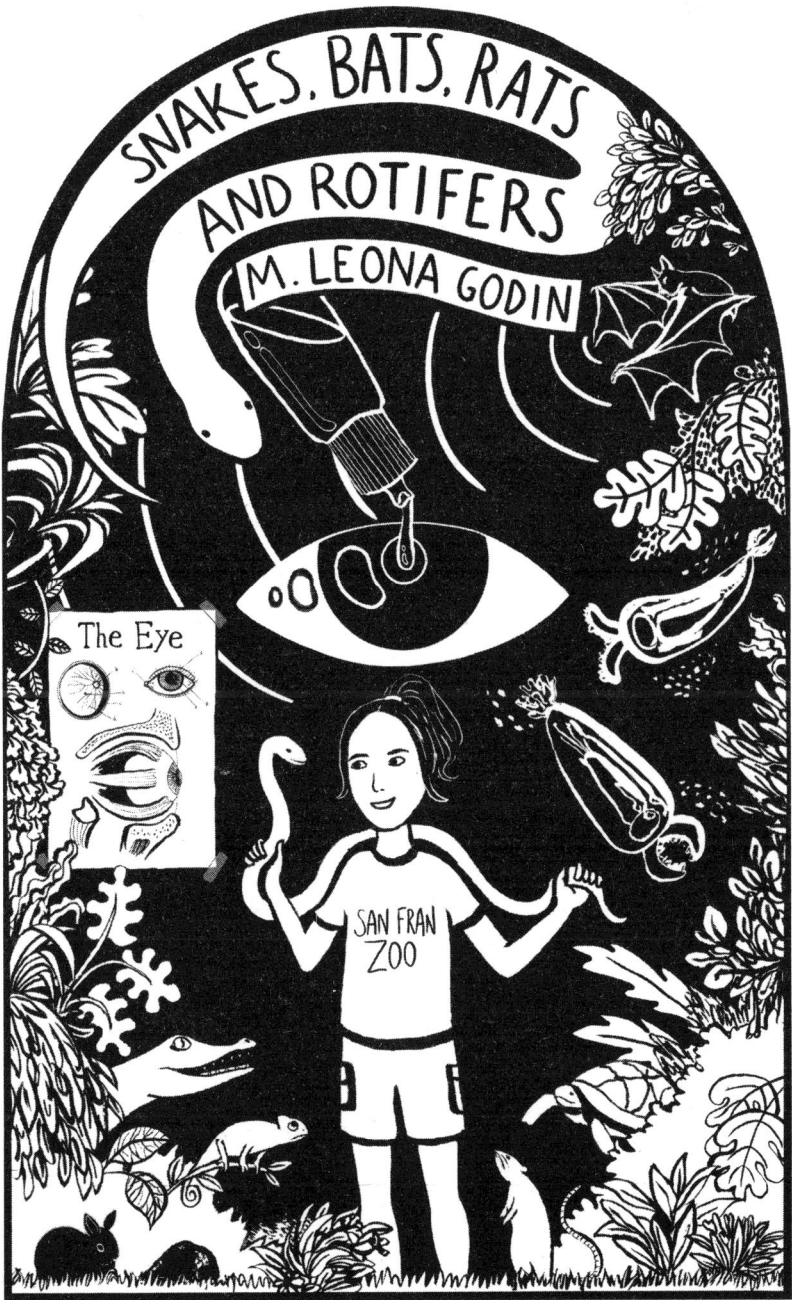

SNAKES, BATS, RATS
AND ROTIFERS
M. LEONA GODIN

The Eye

SAN FRAN
ZOO

Snakes, Bats, Rats and Rotifers

by M. Leona Godin

United States

When I was ten years old, I landed the coolest volunteer job working at the San Francisco Zoo. Every Saturday I presented animals to kids and their parents as they walked along the Nature Trail. I was kind of a know-it-all kid, so it was fun to tell them about (and sometimes let them touch) the animals. There were ferrets and rabbits and skunks – stinky scent glands removed, of course. There was a crow named Jewel and a baby alligator named Charlie. Also turtles – land and aquatic – and lots and lots of snakes. (I loved the snakes.)

I took the bus to the zoo, which was out by the ocean. It was great to walk through the back gate before the visitors arrived. The sounds of the city disappeared and all you could hear were the birds in the rustling cypress and eucalyptus trees that lined the path, the splashes and squabbles of ducks and geese in the pond nearby, and the distant calls of elephants and baboons on the other side of the zoo. Before we took our animals out to the Nature Trail, we had to feed them and clean their cages in the Animal House. This was not the most glamorous part of the job, but it was gratifying in its own way. We removed the pee-soaked, poo-laden wood chips and newspaper scraps and replaced them with fresh, clean-smelling bedding. We filled their bowls with food and their bottles with water.

My eye disease began to present itself during my three years at the zoo. At first it was super subtle, but I did notice some changes, like when I walked from the bright outdoors into the relative dark of the Animal House, my eyes took longer to adjust. For a minute or two, I could hardly see a thing. It startled me at first, but then I figured out that I could keep myself walking straight by paying attention to the glints of light reflecting off the metal cages of the small mammals on my right and the glowing yellow dots of the heat lamps in the reptile section to my left.

The longer I worked at the zoo, the more – and bigger – animals I got trained on. I was so excited when I got trained on Matilda, the boa constrictor. It was really cool to be out on the Nature Trail with that six-foot long, four inches in diameter boa draped around my neck. People stopped dead at fifty paces – and by people, I mean adults.

'Oh no,' they shouted, 'I'm not coming any closer to that thing. It's gonna bite me!'

'Don't worry,' I'd call back with a big smile, 'Matilda won't bite you, she's a constrictor. She strangles her prey!'

I felt so powerful.

***

Once, I was at the rabbit station with Little Joe. Little Joe was a Netherland Dwarf rabbit with very pretty deep grey fur and super-soft little bunny ears. It was a chilly afternoon and there were hardly any visitors. The famous San Francisco fog was rolling in off the ocean. Little Joe and I were shivering in our respective corners. Every five minutes, I checked the time on my Swatch – that was a playfully colourful kind of watch that we all had back in the days when watches only told time! It was almost the end of my shift, and the minutes were crawling.

Finally, a woman and her son came up and I started my spiel: 'This is Little Joe. He's a Netherland Dwarf rabbit, so yes, even though he looks like a baby, he's full grown! The Netherland Dwarf is one of the smallest breeds of rabbits, weighing only one-and-a-half to two-and-a-half pounds. Little Joe is four years old and the average lifespan for Nether—'

The woman interrupted, 'But where's the rabbit?'

I gestured to my left and said, 'Right over there.'

She said, 'That's a rock.'

Back when I had low vision, if I knew what something was, I could actually see it better. This is because seeing doesn't just happen in the eyes, it happens in the brain. Sure enough, when I looked back at the rabbit, it was just a rock.

I turned and found Little Joe hiding behind me. I picked him up and offered him to the mother and her kid to pet. But the damage had been done. I felt a deep blush creep from the bottom of my neck to the roots of my hair. I was so ashamed.

Why shame?

I had been caught 'looking blind'. A lot of adults acted like being blind was the worst thing ever. I guess I thought so too, at first.

***

Mom took me to the optometrist to get glasses,

but glasses didn't help. Then she took me to the ophthalmologists. Mom said they had way more education than the optometrists. They had to go to medical school first and then specialise in the eye because the eye is so complex. I was impressed. But they didn't know what was going on with my eyes either.

One doctor said, 'Her body is growing too fast for her eyes.' Or maybe it was: 'Her eyes are growing too fast for her body.'

I remember Mom telling a friend this in the grocery store afterwards. And I thought it was kind of funny. Would my eyes keep growing and growing until I looked like one of those cute cartoon animals with enormous eyes framed by pretty long lashes? That didn't sound so bad.

***

Soon my mom and I found ourselves face to face with the head of the ophthalmology department. He didn't have an answer to explain my poor eyesight either. I think it frustrated him to not know. He sent me out of the room to wait outside his office.

The door was cracked open, and I was all ears, like a guard-dog pup. But I could not protect my mom from the doctor's meanness.

He told her that there was nothing wrong with my eyes.
'Maybe she can't see because you've been taking her to
so many eye doctors.'

He was scolding her. It made me feel sorry for her and
angry with him. I heard tears in Mom's voice when she
asked: 'Then why can't she read the writing on the
board?'

Somehow her earnest question caused the doctor
to call me back. He looked into my eyes with his
ophthalmoscope – that's like a small hand-held
microscope that shows the back of the eye, which is
called the retina. He saw some spots of discolouration
that caused him to re-evaluate the situation.

The doctor never apologised, but he certainly started
taking an interest. Testing would reveal that the bits
of discolouration meant that the light-sensing cells –
photoreceptors – had begun to die. He said I had a rare
progressive eye disease.

'It progresses differently in different people,' he told us.
'Sometimes it stabilises for years. Eventually, however,
she'll probably be totally blind.'

My mom didn't use the B-word, though. It scared her
too much. Because the prognosis seemed kind of vague,

she ran with it and told people: 'The doctors don't know much about it. It could get worse. It could stay the same. It could even get better.'

I'm pretty sure the doctors did not say that last bit, but it made us feel better. Or at least it made her feel better. I refused to think about my future blindness. It seemed too far away – like adulthood itself – far away and incomprehensible. Instead of worrying about what might happen to my eyes someday, I could learn what was happening right then.

***

In school we were supposed to give a report on an animal. It could be any animal. My friends chose zebras or elephants or horses, lions or dogs or parrots. I chose the rotifer. What's a rotifer, you ask?

That's what everybody asked, and (just like at the zoo) I loved telling them: 'A rotifer is a microscopic animal that lives in ponds and lakes. The rotifer is named for the wheel-like shape of its head that boasts lots of cilia – little hairs – that wave food bits into its mouth.'

I had seen a photo of a rotifer in my textbook, and it caught my imagination. It delighted me to research this tiny creature that people didn't even know existed, that people couldn't see with their naked eye. It glowed in the light of the microscope and looked so alien. An alien among us, unseen and special. Unique. And people with perfectly functioning eyes could never see it without help, without magnification. Without technology.

***

I began to not always feel ashamed of my eye disease – my rare eye disease. In a way, it kind of made me feel special. That feeling of specialness increased exponentially when the scientists at a research institute asked me to have my eyes tested using their cutting-edge, experimental gadgets.

Mom said, 'You don't have to do it if you don't want to.'

I told her I did. I thought it would be interesting. 'I can make a class presentation!'

Every day for a whole week, instead of going to school, Mom took me to the research laboratory to be a subject. Basically, I was a very special lab rat.

I have to admit that my first task as a lab rat was disappointing. The research assistant asked me to put a whole bunch of little coloured discs in a rainbow order: blues with blues, greens with greens, and so on. Some discs were highly pigmented – a dark red, for example – and others were very light, like a pale pink. There were sooo many shades, like way more than a box of Crayola crayons. Until then, I didn't realise I was sort of colourblind, and I got frustrated. Blues and greens and even some purples all kind of looked alike to me, although I could certainly see that the pinks and oranges and reds were something else. This was because of those dying photoreceptors. Some of them are called cones and they help humans see colour.

Things got more fun with the visual field test. I imagined how I'd present it to my class: 'For the visual field test, I had to stare straight into a machine that looked like a brightly lit toilet bowl! It had a blue light in the centre. While keeping my eyes focused on that centre dot, I was supposed to push a button when I saw a red light appear elsewhere on the screen.'

Then, as now, a presentation has a hard time getting some people's attention without good visuals, so I was glad when they told me they'd be taking photos of the back of my eye. In order to do this, they put a needle in my arm – as if they were taking blood – but instead of the liquid blood going out the tube, fluorescent yellow dye was going out of a tube and into my veins. The technician told me that it would only take a few minutes for my heart to pump the dye into the blood vessels at the back of my eye making everything more easily seen. When that happened, she took pictures. I stared straight ahead and tried to keep from blinking at the super-bright flashes. That was a little bit hard, but it was worth it to have the retina selfies! They looked like glowing pastel-coloured planets.

Unfortunately, I forgot to take a picture of my fluorescent yellow pee!

On the last day of testing, they dilated my eyes, which means they put drops in my eyes to make the pupils really big. Also anaesthetising drops to make me not feel anything. Then they put these giant contact lenses on my eyeballs that had wires sticking out of them from all directions. Yep, that meant I couldn't blink the whole time. Did you know that the cells in your body carry a tiny electric charge? I didn't know until they told me that this test with the wacky contacts measured the electrical signals of the cells in my retina.

After I presented my class my story of being a lab rat and told my jokes and showed my pictures, the teacher said, 'Thank you for your presentation. That was fascinating.'

And my friends said: 'That was cool!' 'Were you scared?' 'The photos of your eyeballs look sci-fi!' 'You really couldn't blink for all that time?'

I liked answering their questions and talking about my eye disease. It made me feel different in a good way. And knowing a little bit about my eye disease made me feel like I had the power to choose how to present myself and my story. I wasn't just losing sight; I was becoming blind.

***

I'm way older now, and I am totally blind. Even though some people still think it's the worst thing ever, being blind is not a big deal. I have good days and bad, just like everyone else. In fact, a lot of things are easier now than when I was a kid because I have all kinds of accessible technology that makes it possible for me to read and to be writing these words to you.

One thing that hasn't changed is that I still love animals. These days my favourites are bats. Did you know that bats are the second-largest order of mammals after rodents? There are all kinds of bats, and they live all over the world. Some bats are big and prefer eating sweet things like fruits and nectar. Some bats are small and prefer the bitter spiciness of bugs. Some bats use echolocation to fly through the night sky. That means instead of using their eyes to navigate, they use their ears! They make sounds – like clicks and ultrasonic shouts – that bounce off objects in the world and return to them as echoes. Bugs reflect sound differently than trees do.

Blind people can also use echolocation to navigate. It's a different way of doing things, and it works pretty well. I'm learning how to echolocate using clicks and listening hard. It takes a lot of practice. I wish my kid know-it-all self could have learned how to do it. But people didn't talk about it or teach it back then. I think if I had known, it would have made me proud of what I was becoming. Plus, I would have had great material for a killer presentation. No visuals necessary.

GROWING PAINS

CHRISTA COUTURE

Growing Pains

by Christa Couture

Canada

I always knew I was destined for the stage.

I wanted to be on Broadway. I would be in *Cats*, *Phantom of the Opera*, *Annie*, *Sound of Music*, *Into the Woods* – all the musicals I knew by heart before I was ten. I would be Julie Andrews, Bette Midler, Bernadette Peters.

'A triple threat' – I learned the term early on: a triple threat was a performer who could sing, act and dance. Those three skills became my Broadway-bound to-do list.

The singing part was a no-brainer. I'd been singing from as soon as I could talk. As a Cree person, I was given my traditional name at age four. Traditional names are given during a naming ceremony or by family and are different from legal names given at birth. My traditional name was Singing Woman. The elder who performed my naming ceremony told my family, 'She's going to sing a lot, and she's going to talk a lot.'

Whenever my family would hear me singing – in the car, in my room, while they sat assembled on the couch for my latest 'production,' or while we sang together – they would remind me lovingly, 'Oh, we were told you would sing a lot and you would talk a lot! Our Singing Woman.'

I learned all the songs I loved, and I also wrote songs from as early as I can remember. When I was eight, two friends and I wrote three original songs and asked if we could perform them in front of the entire school.

We made a backdrop from a huge cardboard box, drawing a landscape on it with crayons. We even made custom shirts to perform in – white short-sleeve sweatshirts with iron-on puffy pink paint that had our band name emblazoned across the front: **Krazy Kids**.

Nervously we stood in front of the school, 150 students seated on the gymnasium floor, folded our arms across our chest, counted ourselves in and sang, a cappella: **'My crazy kid has gooo-ooone, uh oh, uh oh, she's gone one mile, uh oh, uh oh, she's gone two miles** . . .' How many miles did we sing until we stopped flapping our arms and turning around? I don't know. I thought I might faint from the butterflies flapping in my stomach, and my voice cracked ever so slightly (**did anyone hear?! How embarrassing!**) but the moment it was done, the nervous energy instantly transformed into triumph: we did it!

And I wanted to do it again. To stand in front of an audience and give them a show. Even though the older rows of kids at the back of the gym had rolled their eyes and snickered, there was enough applause from the rest of the grades to make it a well-received performance. Truthfully, it wouldn't have taken much to be 'enough' – the passion to perform was an easily stoked fire in my chest.

I joined a girls' choir. Every Thursday evening, I took the bus downtown and learned songs arranged for three-part harmonies, soprano, second-soprano and alto.

My best friend Susan became my musical co-conspirator. We wrote, composed, built sets, designed costumes and performed one-act plays in my basement rec room, usually for an audience of our parents and one of their friends, maybe a neighbour, and, once, our school teacher even came! We arranged two-part harmonies for every song we knew, passing the time in car rides and backyards, singing for hours.

So, singing has always been one of my greatest joys – and natural abilities. First 'threat' of the Triple Threat: check.

Then there was the acting. Theatrics came easily, but the discipline to learn lines and study character was hard work – 'Acting Woman' was **not** my traditional name, to be sure.

I enrolled in an evening drama class and met David McNally – a charismatic, enthusiastic **Man of the Stage**. We'd enter the room and he would be lying on the floor on his back doing vocal exercises. He seemed eccentric and bold, **a real artist!** I studied him as a person as closely as I listened to his guidance. My favourite character development was to decide which body part would lead when I walked – did my character lead with their stomach? Their chin? Their left elbow? I memorised lines and imagined backstories.

Second threat of the Triple Threat: working on it.

One of Susan's greatest joys and natural abilities was dance. She was the choreographer for our productions and would share with me what she learned at her latest ballet or contemporary dance class. The first time I saw a production of *The Nutcracker*, I thought ballet might be the path for me, too, but mostly I wanted the cute outfits. Once enrolled in ballet, there weren't enough cute costumes to hold my interest and the rules of movement felt restrictive. **Meh**, Susan could teach me! And I'd keep my physical chops developed in gymnastics. Running, jumping, swinging! Cartwheels and hanging upside down! Gymnastics was like dance-meets-tree-climbing, and maybe I wouldn't be the kind of dancer to be cast in *Cats*, but I could be a mover great enough for many other musicals, I was sure.

Besides, the ingénue doesn't need to be **as** good a dancer as the chorus line.

Third threat of the Triple Threat: close enough.

***

I was living in Edmonton, Alberta, Canada, with my mom and sister. My world revolved around choir, piano practice and drama class. By nine years old, I saw my path clearly – I would be singing, acting and dancing (ish) for audiences hundreds of times larger than the basement rec room productions.

In the summer of being ten, I started to feel a pain in my left leg: at first an ache from deep within, then, over a few weeks, the pain became sharper and more constant. It hurt to walk; it wasn't much more comfortable to sit still.

'Growing pains!' my dad assessed at first, but after more

than a month of pain, we noticed a large lump on my leg.

The first doctor I went to thought it might be a spider bite. My family had been camping on the East Coast – **very different spiders there than in the prairies!** we figured. I was put on antibiotics and sent home.

The pain continued.

The next doctor suggested I get an X-ray. That X-ray revealed it wasn't the work of a mysterious Eastern Seaboard spider, it was a tumour. I would have to be admitted to the hospital for more tests.

On the day of the tests, I was supposed to go to school first, and we'd head to the hospital after. I rode my bike on the familiar path from my house to school and joined the routine of my grade five class. But I felt a pit in my stomach. What was wrong with my leg? What would happen at the hospital? What would the tests feel like? How long would it take?

I remember the ride home: a beautiful October afternoon with trees dressed in all their fall beauty. I looked up at the sky. I sang to myself. In so many ways, it was the same as every other regular ride. When I parked my bike in the garage, I didn't know I wouldn't get to ride it again.

It took many days of tests – X-rays, bone scans, CT-scans, an MRI and finally a biopsy – to get the news: I had bone cancer.

I barely knew what cancer was, though I remembered the word from my Uncle Dennis' death a few years earlier. Even though he had died, the seriousness of the illness didn't fully register. It may be that no one explained it fully to me; my family worked hard to stay positive for me but may have unintentionally hindered my understanding in doing so. As far as I knew, I was sick, but I'd get better.

Once the doctors knew it was cancer, they wanted to act quickly. I had surgery to place a catheter in my chest, which is like a semi-permanent IV to get the medicine through, and I began chemotherapy and radiotherapy.

Chemotherapies are strong drugs – drugs that make you intensely sick to your stomach and make your hair fall out. For a year and a half, I spent one week of every month in the hospital getting this treatment.

For six weeks during that year I had radiotherapy, which is radiation: high-energy particles, aimed at an isolated part of the body to kill malignant cancer cells. In my case, it was aimed at my lower left leg where the tumour was. Radiotherapy didn't make me sick, so I could still go to school after early morning treatments. But, in the precise rectangle where they targeted the rays, my leg got a serious burn, as if I'd fallen asleep in the sun for days with just that part showing.

During these treatments, even though I **could** walk, I was told not to. Where the tumour was growing, my fibula – my calf bone – was becoming weak. If I did a lot of walking (not to mention running, jumping or getting back on my bike), I risked breaking the bone.

I used a wheelchair at school. I sat on the side throughout gym classes. I watched my friends move freely across the schoolyard during recess. I felt left out and isolated, but made light of my bald head to ease the discomfort of my peers and let them take turns at trying my wheelchair. At home I walked, but used crutches to limit impact on the bone.

Eventually, it became clear the treatments weren't working. The tumour had shrunk at first, but the effect was short term.

The only option left was to amputate my leg above the knee. Over dinner, my mom gave me the news. I poked my spaghetti for a moment, not looking up, and then said, 'Bummer,' before taking another bite. I felt like everything was exploding, but I pushed the feelings away and fought to not get emotional.

'I'll just get a fake leg, right?' I asked.

'Yes,' my mom replied slowly. I shrugged to try and hide how overwhelmed I felt, wanting it to be as simple as 'just' anything.

That was a Thursday evening and the surgery would be the following Wednesday, the day after my thirteenth birthday. It gave us little time to get used to the idea.

I stood in front of a full-length mirror, trying to balance on my right leg while holding my left leg bent behind me. I wanted to envision what I would look like with a stump. I couldn't look for long.

That weekend, I had an urgently rescheduled birthday party with my two closest friends. We danced to the *Little Mermaid* soundtrack in my basement and I felt a panic and fear start to grow in my chest. What would it feel like to not be able to do this again, like this, on two legs, in this body? I couldn't compute the loss and change ahead of me. I pushed the thoughts away.

But it still happened. The day after my thirteenth

birthday, I went into the hospital for that surgery.

***

Becoming disabled didn't mean I understood what had happened to me. I didn't come out of hospital knowing the words 'amputee' or 'disabled'. All I knew was that I was missing even more school, that I was in even more pain, and that I had to learn to walk again on an artificial leg. It's a good thing we don't remember learning to walk as toddlers, because it's not easy!

'Can amputees dance?' I asked my physiotherapist, one day. I was standing on a trampoline and she had a belt tied around my waist to catch me when I started to fall over. Which I did, because she was bouncing me on a trampoline. Honestly, the question was premature. I couldn't yet walk without holding on to a person, a wall or a cane, and I was months away from being able to wear my prosthesis for a full day, but my focus was singular: I wanted to be a performer.

'Of course they can!' she replied encouragingly.

Perhaps she didn't know I meant to dance **professionally**. Perhaps she didn't want to dissuade me from pursuing my goals. But her optimism fed the stubborn thought in my head that I could still be on Broadway.

Sure, I'd missed out on a couple years of dancing and acting classes, and, OK, yes, I now only had one leg, which was indisputably a challenge to becoming a Triple Threat . . . But my singing voice remained as strong as ever.

I was determined that I could **make it**.

***

In Alberta, you change schools at grade ten and enter high school, and at fifteen I enrolled in **the** performing arts school in town. They had a beautiful 685-seat proper theatre. They had drama, musical theatre, voice, dance, every kind of class for every kind of performer headed for the stage. They produced a play and a dance show and a musical each year.

In my first year there, the school was mounting a production of *The Threepenny Opera*. I sang 'Gus: The Theatre Cat' from *Cats* for my audition, one of the young, brave new students hoping for a part. That audition was just in front of three teachers.

But then I got a callback audition. Yeee! And **that** was in front of everyone who was being considered for the production: my fellow grade ten students, all of us in varying degrees of awe and terror, and the more experienced grade elevens and twelves. Oh, the grade twelve students! So much older at seventeen and eighteen. So much cooler. So knowing and aware.

At the callbacks, I was asked to sing for one of the lead roles, Mrs Peachum. A few of the grade twelves came up to me after: 'Grade tens **never** get auditioned for lead roles – that was so lucky! You can't get the part, but just wait 'til you're in grade twelve, you'll be the lead for sure.'

I blushed a little and beamed to know I had been an exception.

And I learned they were right: grade tens **didn't** ever get cast in lead roles – the thinking being that each student spends a couple years developing, and then gets their turn at a starring part in their final year at the school. Less a system of 'the best person for the part' and more 'we're all learning and they're just kids'. I was cast in the chorus. I had a fantastic time.

In grade eleven, I continued to take all the classes and sing in all the choirs. I learned about a famous one-legged tap dancer named Peg Leg Bates and went to the library to find out more (these days, I could just look up Evan Ruggiero on YouTube). I even brought my physiotherapist to one of my musical theatre classes so she could help me learn how to adapt the dance moves I couldn't do and practise the ones I could. It took me a lot longer to learn the choreography – because you can't feel a prosthetic limb, you must watch and repeat the moves in a way that helps you memorise what to do, without feeling.

To be honest, most of the moves weren't something I could learn, not because my brain didn't understand them, but because my one-legged body simply could not physically do what a two-legged body could. Does that seem obvious? It wasn't to me. I wanted it too badly.

Being in denial of my new reality was starting to take its toll. In front of the full wall mirror during class, I began to struggle not to cry as I watched my peers move and twist and leap around me while I thudded clumsily on my prosthesis. I began to resent seeing my reflection in the mirror, my body moving so differently from everyone else's.

'You can't dance like them, it's true, but you can sing circles around every single one of them,' my musical theatre teacher consoled me.

I held on to my strengths, believing they were enough to

keep going. At seventeen, I started grade twelve poised for my moment. Bette Midler. Bernadette Peters. Julie Andrews. **Here I come**.

That year, the school chose to produce *Crazy For You*. I already knew the song – and I'd seen the musical during a summer trip to New York. Who doesn't love a Gershwin tune?

I would be a wonderful Polly – the lead, the ingénue, the one who gets to sing 'Embrace me, my sweet embraceable you.' But . . . *Crazy For You* is a very dance-heavy musical, and not just for the chorus parts. The leads **have** to dance.

Surely, the directors would figure out how to make it work for me. Surely. I'd done everything my teachers and peers had told me to do for three years, holding on to their promise of a lead role. I'd been working towards that senior year like it was the end of my life. I'd followed the path laid out for me to make it from new student to star of the show.

I refused to consider it wouldn't work out. I refused to believe that my recently acquired disability would keep me from my dream. I refused to believe those in charge wouldn't make accommodations for me.

The day of the *Crazy For You* auditions came. I practised my sixteen-bar song audition for my musical theatre teacher. I nailed it. She hugged me. 'I'm so proud of you!'

She wasn't going to be part of the team directing *Crazy For You*, but she told me, 'You won't have to do the dance portion of the audition. They know about your leg, and they will work with you. Just do your song and your monologue, and that's all you have to do.'

But that afternoon, in the theatre, among the crowds of students that were being herded into different groups and different lines for different parts of the group audition process, I found myself suddenly thrust onto the stage and into the lights . . . in a dance line-up.

I stood, frozen. I heard the choreographer start to shout the routine, and with a 'five, six, seven, eight' four lines of teenagers started executing the moves. I got bumped into. I bumped into others. I tried to keep up in some way but got pushed into the wings. **How did I get in the dance group? They told me I wouldn't have to?**

Tears started to well up inside. I covered my eyes to see who was sitting in the audience, to see if one of the teachers I knew was there, someone to say, 'It's OK, you don't have to do this part.' I didn't recognise anybody.

'Next group!' the choreographer shouted, and I was shuffled into another room with the crowd. It was time to sing.

Tears running down my cheeks, trying to catch my breath, I walked in and sang my sixteen bars – ironically, of the song 'The Music That Makes Me Dance' (learned from the 1964 recording with Barbra Streisand). It was half as good as what I'd done earlier that day, but I made it through.

I sobbed as I walked to the bus stop. I heaved tears and snotty, choking breaths the whole ride home. I walked through our door and continued to sob, trying to tell my mom what happened.

'They . . . put . . . me . . . in . . . the . . . dance . . . group,' heave, heave, choke, cry.

The tears, I know now, weren't just for that night. For three years, I'd been so determined to carry on. But determination can be denial – grief hiding itself in a fixed purpose. I thought about what I wanted – Broadway – so that I didn't have to think about what I didn't want. I didn't want to be disabled. I didn't want to look different or move differently. I didn't want things to have changed.

But things **had** changed. I'd lost my leg, yes. But I'd also lost the future I had always imagined.

I was heartbroken.

***

The next day, I was called into the vice principal's office. I was even pulled out in the middle of writing an exam to go talk to her. 'I heard about what happened yesterday. I'm so sorry. The directors knew about your leg, you should not have been put in that group. They were impressed you tried anyway!' she added, trying to give some sort of 'bright side', I suppose. But all I could think then, and all I can think now, is that someone should have helped me. Someone should have said, 'You don't have to try this.' They should have said it at the audition; they should have said it earlier. They had three years of high school to say it. But maybe they were sold on the idea that I could 'overcome' my disability, just as I was. It would have made a good story.

Here's what I know now. Pushing past our limits is not always necessary; knowing what we can't do is not defeat.

The directors cast me in the chorus, and, scandalously (as far as high school musical scandals go), they cast a grade ten student in the lead role of Polly.

I turned down the chorus part and stopped listening to my musical theatre soundtracks. I cried. I felt terrible. I felt bitter and sad and disappointed and like I didn't know what to dream about anymore.

I would never make it to Broadway, and it took me a while to come to terms with that and to find a new version of pursuing my passions in a way that was realistic for my disability.

After high school I moved from that prairie town to the west coast city of Vancouver. I started guitar lessons. I started writing more and more of my own songs. I started performing my songs at open-mic nights. I started playing gigs in front of audiences. I recorded my first album, then my second, all the way up to my seventh. I toured across Canada, Germany, the Netherlands and England. Over ten years, I had countless meaningful, beautiful, glorious experiences as a performer.

It may not have been what I first imagined, and while I wasn't a triple threat, the stage did prove to be my destiny. So I wasn't wrong about that, at least. And neither was the elder who'd named me: I was – I am – Singing Woman, after all.

Naughty or Sick?

by Jessica Kellgren-Fozard

United Kingdom

We had come to an uneasy truce, Miss Hill and I.

Me: slightly jaded eight-year-old who could be inexplicably injured by a pile of leaves.

She: primary school receptionist, head's assistant, administrator, disciplinarian, music teacher, occasional dinner lady and nurse (this school really should have hired more people).

Neither of us enjoyed seeing each other.

Poor Miss Hill. When she signed on for first-aid training, she can't have been expecting to deal with a child whose limbs stubbornly refused to stay in their sockets, who got sick with every bug going, tripped over leaves in the playground and had managed to fall down every single step in the whole school at least five times in her first year there.

So, she might not have been expecting to deal with me. But she had to, and far more frequently than she wished to.

Understandably, her face changed in the first couple of years, from sympathy to a pressed 'could you at least be quiet this time?' as she silently made me wiggle my limbs and follow her finger with my eyes.

There is probably a spot in your primary school that you remember best: Under the big tree? Hopscotch? The art room? Mine is the three hard, bobbly, honestly quite putrid-smelling faux-woollen chairs that lined the corridor between Miss Hill's office door and the headmistress's.

Fall over in the playground? Sit on the chairs.

Push someone over in the playground? Sit on the chairs.

Which made anyone sitting on the chairs an object of rabid fascination for any child walking through the main corridor.

Why exactly were you sitting on the chairs today? What villainous crime had you committed? What terrible plague were you spreading? Who were you there to see?

'Naughty or sick?'

'Naughty or sick?'

I would shuffle up to Miss Hill's office, stumbling along and clutching whatever floppy limb it was this time, tears streaking down my face. After a resigned, 'What's wrong now?' she would leave me to slump down in my chairs (clearly I had a sense of ownership by this point) and fill out my latest incident report – number 1109: 'PE. Badminton. Mr Stevens says I am probably the only person in the world to ever be injured by a shuttlecock.' (Though I'd argue it was actually **the ground** hitting me that hurt.)

Then I would sit there and stare up until I had managed to count through all 326 ceiling tiles. Twice . . . And then shuffle back to class.

Perhaps you are asking, 'Didn't Miss Hill provide first-aid care?'

No. Of course she didn't. She was the school receptionist. What was she going to do?!

***

When I was born the doctor handed me to my parents and said, 'There's something wrong with this one but we can't tell what, it will probably emerge in time.'

Helpful.

I was still waiting for an actual diagnosis (other than 'clumsy', 'lazy', 'scatterbrained', 'accident-prone', 'ditzy', 'a nuisance' or 'I really don't have time for this right now') when, on the morning of 24th March 1997, I made a terrible mistake.

My mother dropped me off early before school started and I, somehow forgetting everything I knew about myself, jumped right into playing a game of Doctor-Doctor with half of my class.

For those who aren't familiar with my school's version of Doctor-Doctor, it involves contorting your body into strange positions, then clasping hands with the contorted people next to you until you have created a ring of people waiting to be unwound by 'The Doctor'. It looks ridiculous and it is a **terrible** idea.

We played it on the concrete paving.

Yes, dear reader, I am sure you can see where this is going.

So there I am, both hands between my legs, each grabbing on to a different friend, staring down at the concrete and letting my mind wander . . . not really thinking about anything . . . when suddenly – **WHOOM!** – a sharp pull on my right arm and, with no hand to save me, the concrete floor is racing towards my shoulder and my face . . .

CRACK!

Black. Black. Black.

Is my nose still sticking out?

Blue. Blue. Blue.

The sky so blue.

The wood of the trellis.

A blinking ring of faces.

Oh, hello, Redhead New Lady Teacher, what are you— NO! DON'T TOUCH MY ARM! OOOOOOOOOW!!!

'Eeewww,' said Michael.

Now there is vomit all over her shoe and this awful, awful noise. A building scream of primal pain. Oh, it's me. I'm screaming.

I can't seem to turn it off.

Weirdly, in all my many, many times falling down staircases, I had only experienced a rather dull pain before, like being hit with something round. A nice, round mallet, maybe. But this was shockingly different.

It was pointed, spiky: excruciating.

Oh God, I'm being murdered!

The teacher's face looms again, she narrows her eyes then rolls them, motioning around. 'She won't stop screaming and it's distressing the other children.' Who's she talking to? Oh good, it's Mr Carpenter.

Mr Carpenter is the best, nicest, warmest, friendliest janitor ever and he's trying extra hard to carry me gently, but I think I might still be sick on him. He puts my head on his shoulder and the dragging feeling at the back of my skull eases off . . . So that's good. But I'm cradling my right arm, which somehow feels too heavy to hold and not in any way attached . . . Yep, definitely going to be sick on him. **Blugh!** Sorry, Mr Carpenter.

'What's wrong now?' asks Miss Hill.

The floppy dead weight hanging from the shards of what used to be my shoulder? 'My arm.'

A sigh. 'Fine, I'll ring your mother.'

'Thank you.' Vomit. 'Ouch.'

'Oh, and here's a bucket.'

She hands me an old ice-cream tub. It still smells faintly of chemical vanilla.

The edge of my vision is purple, I think, or black or blue or gr— **blugh!** 'Ouch.' And I can't focus on my normally-so-relaxing ceiling tiles. But I try.

'Well, I left her a message. Seems there wasn't anyone home. Do you think you can go back to class while we wait for her? It's almost time for assembly.'

I fly forwards like a rag doll in a convulsion of vomit. Too much staring at the ceiling tiles.

'I suppose not, then. OK, just wait there. I'll be in the office if you need me.'

The chair is scratchy against my face and it smells like vanilla now too. Where's my mummy? Where is that terrible ringing noise coming from? I've turned to jelly and sticky pain, like gloopy jam that never rubs off. I think my bones might be in pieces and floating separately around the goo.

Is this death?

God, no. I'm not allowing that to happen. I've never even been to Disneyland!

The ringing sound again, but louder. Hundreds of tiny feet patter past me. I'm still in the main corridor. They're all going to assembly. I try to call for help. It's just a groan. I try to reach out a sticky hand . . .

'Are you naughty or sick?' ask dozens of tiny faces.

Isn't it obvious, dumdum!?

'Naughty or sick?'

'Stop looking in the sick bucket, Samuel!'

No! Come back and look in my sick bucket, Samuel! Then go and get my mummy!

'Walk on, please! Leave her alone!'

No, don't leave me alone! At least can someone please help me go to the toilet? I really need to go and it's along this corridor and up the wide stairs and . . . along a whole other corridor . . .

Please help!

But that's just a groan and all of those fuzzy faces are going now. I can hear Mrs Edmonds starting assembly and then the swing doors close.

Mummy? I really need to go to the toilet.

Big girls of eight do **not** wet themselves. It doesn't matter how much pain I'm in, how blurry my vision is or how much of my sick is currently coating the general area, I haven't wet myself in school for two years at least and I'm **not** going back! Maybe if I lift my head? **Ough!** No. Searing pain. That's a no. Can I stand up? **Blugh!** OK. Can't do that either.

I'm going to have to get there lying down.

Slide off the chairs . . . Don't open your eyes.

Good arm down . . . feel for the floor . . . lower your legs . . . ease your body off . . . hold the useless arm . . . **oof!**

Did it!

Successfully on the floor. Today isn't going so badly after all.

Going to need to take the bucket, though.

Tuck the bucket in the elbow of the sore arm. Use the good hand to hold the bad hand then rest my forehead on it. OK, I can do this.

Bum in the air like a caterpillar and push off!

Ow! No. No. No. Shoulder pain, shoulder pain!

Forget caterpillars! I'm allergic to caterpillars anyway.

Knees to the sides like a frog, push with feet like you're swimming?

No! Ouch. Ouch. Ouch. Head pain. And shoulder pain. Bad frogs.

OK, push out your good elbow and pull back?

That's right, commando crawl. You're doing it! Excellent!

Great.

Good.

Okay.

Drag,

Drag,

Drag . . .

I'm getting there.

Almost to the end.

Almost at the stairs.

I can do this. Hold on. **Blugh!**

Puke Stop at the bottom of the stairs. The wide, shallow stairs . . . If they were steeper, maybe I could just throw myself up them in one big burst of pain and be done with it? This is going to be slow.

Bucket. Arm. Pull.

Bucket. Arm. Pull.

Bucket. Arm. Pain.

Whoops! Almost dropped the bucket. That was a close one, Mr Carpenter! He really is a lovely caretaker.

Bucket. Arm. Pull.

Bucket. Arm. Pull.

Bucket. Arm. Pull.

For one dreadful moment I see-saw back and forth at the top . . . and then . . . **FLOP** . . . I've made it! And the sick bucket goes flying.

That's going to stain. So sorry, Mr Carpenter. You really are a lovely caretaker.

It's easier without the sick bucket, just a slow, sickly, gummy crawl along the corridor of classrooms. Every room has a glass door and I can see the teachers' shoes as I slither past. I am not a caterpillar, or a frog. I am a slug. A sticky, slimy, gross, awful slug.

'Hello?'

Oh hello. You're someone's mummy. Someone in my class – one of the boys who can't read well. You help the teacher sometimes.

'Oh dear, you're not very well are you?'

You've got little children too and you came on the trip to the Roman baths with us.

'What are you doing here?'

I like you.

'Are you OK?'

I gurgle something.

'Oh, sweetheart, shall I help you up? Are you going to the toilet?'

I think you might be God.

She lifts me very gently and cradles my arm like a baby. My sick is on her but she doesn't say anything or even seem to mind. When we get to the toilet she doesn't say anything about my knickers being pink and flowery and maybe a bit little-girlie for someone who is eight. She makes me think that I'm not naughty, that I might actually be sick.

She helps me back along the corridor, down the stairs to the chairs, checks Miss Hill has rung my mother and goes back to her classroom. Definitely need a nap now.

'Naughty or sick?'

It's noisy again when I wake up. They're all going to lunch (what happened to break time?) and staring into the new bowl next to me.

'Um . . . sick.'

'Naughty or sick?'

'Whatever.'

***

When I next wake, the headmistress is looming over me.

'Lunchtime is over now.' (What happened to lunchtime?) 'You've missed the whole morning, why don't you try doing the afternoon?'

'My arm hurts.' It really does. And I need my other hand to hold it close.

Miss Hill is there, too. 'Yes, but your arm hurt last week, didn't it, Jessica, and then it was better by the next day.'

That's not true. I just took the sling off because I had art and it was getting in the way.

'Let's get you back to class.'

I'm crying, but only because it hurts. At least I'm not being sick anymore. And when I swing my legs down, I find I can stand.

We walk through the imposing assembly hall and down the corridor to my classroom. Walking is hard. Everything is fuzzy . . . and dark . . . and the edges are black . . . They walk behind and in front of me like my jailors.

Everyone stays quiet as we enter the classroom. They all stare at me. I'm crying again because it all hurts just too, too much and I really do want my mummy.

'What did she do?' 'Why is she crying?' 'What's wrong with her?' 'What happened?' 'Are you OK?' 'Eww, is that sick?

'That's enough! Return to your seats.' The headmistress stands behind my empty chair.

A weighty pause. 'And? Are you going to sit down and try, Jessica?'

Try what?

I'm seated at my normal table of four, now. The two adults towering over me. Every other kid in the room has their eyes glued to me too.

It's going to be a while before I can live this one down in the playground.

'Just let go of your arm and pick up the pen. Come on. Try writing with it.'

I'm right-handed. My right. The arm I've been cradling for four hours now.

'Just **try**, Jessica.'

My head thumps more and I really can't see through these tears.

'Come on, Jessica, let's not be silly.'

They aren't going to let me leave unless I do something big. Sorry, arm, it's for your own good . . .

'Jessica, we need to get ba—' I let the arm drop.

'GAAAAAAAAAAAAAAAAAAAAAAAH!'

'OH MY GOD!' Children scatter, pens fly everywhere, Miss Hill tumbles over! My arm hangs by skin! The scream can be heard at the other end of the school!

Still screaming, I projectile vomit across the table.

'Hold your arm, hold your arm!'

Sorry, everyone, but I hope you understand.

'Take her back to the chairs! Oh, dear Lord!'

Worth it.

***

In the end my mother didn't arrive until three o'clock, around six hours after I'd originally hurt myself. The school had only left the one message, which contained no sense of urgency, no need to hurry. I sometimes wonder what my mother thought, on finding the sloppy pile of sickness and concussion that vaguely resembled her daughter, lying on its own in the middle of the corridor. If she was shocked I don't remember it. But then, this wasn't an unusual occurrence.

Would you believe, it took another sixteen years to get a full diagnosis as to why these things were happening to me?

And guess what? It turns out I **was** sick!

Not naughty, after all.

Disabled Heroes

by Eugene Grant

United Kingdom

Who are your heroes?

When I was at school, I was asked to write about my
heroes and role models. I can't remember the list in
full. But I remember choosing two skateboarders.
I wrote their names. Jason Acuña and Pancho
Moler. I wrote them down beside others. Freedom
fighters. Suffragettes. Civil rights activists. The names
you'd expect to find on such a list. With the stroke of a
pen, I made these men members of a special league of
history-defining people.

Not everyone agreed with me. Not everybody recognised
their credentials like I did. My teacher wasn't impressed.
Apparently, skateboarders didn't belong with Dr Martin
Luther King Jr. or Mahatma Gandhi. Those who had
sacrificed everything for justice and equality. Well, I
thought, she's free to write her own list. After all, these
are **my** heroes and role models. And I related to these
skateboarders not just because I was a kid whose entire

world was skateboarding, but because they **looked** like me. Because they had dwarfism. Like me.

I didn't get the chance to explain myself to the teacher back then. So here goes . . .

As a child, I didn't have interests or hobbies. I had loves. I had obsessions. I'd seize upon something. And I'd make it fill my every waking moment. I didn't just skateboard. I'd read skateboard magazines. Watch skateboard videos. Wear skateboard clothes. Play skateboard video games. Hang out at skateboard shops. If I wasn't asleep or at school, odds were that I was out with my skateboard. I even had a tiny toy skateboard to occupy my busy fingers and imagination when I probably should've been studying. This wasn't a passion. It was a religion. It was a way of life.

I loved skateboarding. The feeling of freedom as I cruised along pavements. The **duguh-duguh-duguh-duguh** sound of wheels rolling over the gaps between paving stones. The sense of accomplishment when I landed a new trick after hours, days or weeks of practice. The rush I'd get from throwing myself down a flight of steps or flying off a ramp. That split second of hang time. The buzz of being moved on or even chased by security guards whose job it was to stop kids like me turning their company's HQ or campus into our own concrete playground.

Any kid who's skateboarded will know these feelings. But I experienced something different. Something more. I wasn't just buoyed by my own sense of satisfaction. I was physically **charged** by the turned heads and nods of approval from average height, non-disabled spectators. As a regular teenager, my dwarfism blacklisted me from circles of 'cool' kids at school. But, as a skater with dwarfism, my ability on a board bought me respect from, and a place among, older boys and men. Skateboarding wasn't a hobby. It was my ticket. I was certified. I was a dwarf, sure, but I was decent on a deck.

And so, 'professional skateboarder' became my latest career aspiration. There were others before this. When I was seven, I desperately wanted to be a marine or in the SAS (kind of like our Navy Seals). Again, I didn't just 'play with toy guns', like many kids my age did. I literally ran laps around the school playground at lunchtime in the hope I'd be fit enough to join, once I was old enough. (Yes, I can see how that looks weird now. But you get the point. I **really** wanted to be in the army.)

To be fair, I was never really going to become the smallest ever paid-up member of some armed-to-the-teeth, highly trained special ops squad. Even though, as I said after my first time paintballing, a smaller target is harder to hit. (And, for the record, I didn't get shot once. Ha! Take that, army recruiting office.) So, not long after I started secondary school, I found a new dream. I'd be the first professional dwarf basketball player in the NBA.

At eleven, basketball became the air I breathed. Posters covered my bedroom walls. Replica vests hung in my wardrobe. I devoured *Slam* magazine, reading it cover to cover each month. I bought videos from the USA and watched them until I knew them by heart. I played basketball computer games. A miniature basketball hoop hung on the back of my door. So even just leaving my room provided a chance to fantasise about stunning an imaginary arena of fans with a gravity-defying slam dunk.

Practice makes perfect, right? So, I practised. Oh man, I **practised**. Indoors. Outdoors. In the sun. In the cold. In the machine-gun rain. It didn't matter. That feeling, as that smooth burned orange rubber sphere spun into my palms. An electricity. A caress. A hug. From an old friend. I didn't practise wildly, either. I was deliberate. Intentional. I'd drill the same shot. Again and again. Over and over. Hundreds, maybe thousands, of times.

Until.

I.

Got.

It.

Right.

Because, within all my dreams and fantasies, I knew. I knew the raised eyebrows that came when people saw, for the first time, a body like mine walk onto a basketball court. The reactions of mild to moderate surprise. Low expectations from those who only (wrongly) understood the game as a sport for tall men. I didn't exactly blend in as a dwarf in everyday life. (I would've been a terrible spy – another surrendered dream.) Yet here I was, trespassing in the land of giants. I knew how good I'd have to be to disprove doubters. To show these people that this dwarf had **game**. I wasn't a pity pick. Blink, and I will **destroy you**.

I tell you what, though – being small had some real advantages. At three-foot-eleven, I could dribble the ball so low to the ground, tall players would struggle to reach it. Being taken less seriously meant people often didn't notice me. I'd race up behind them. Out of sight. Steal the ball from under them. And dash away while they stood there, blinking, unsure of what had just happened. I liked nothing better than making a bigger player marking me think I was about to go to their left. Then, at the last minute, go right. There was something righteous about putting the ball between their legs. Spinning around them. And collecting it on their other side. Beating taller kids wasn't enough. I wanted to be so good I'd **embarrass** them.

But still, no matter how good I was no one else seemed to think that a kid with dwarfism might make it to the NBA. Not that far. Not **really**. I mean, after all, nobody had done it before. It'd be many more years before Jahmani Swanson – who has the same condition I have, achondroplasia – would don a Harlem Globetrotters jersey.

'You could be a great coach,' those close to me insisted. They said it with a care. A kindness. An honesty. But the meaning was unmistakable: **This? This here? Even with all that you have done. As hard as you have worked. It will never be enough. I am sorry. But this is something you will never have . . . Maybe not today. Maybe not tomorrow. But, sometime, you will have to let it go. You know that . . . Don't you?**

A few years later, and now officially a teenager, seeing those two skateboarders whose dwarf bodies looked like my dwarf body, I knew things could be different this time. I wouldn't have to bulldoze my way through walls of disbelief. This time, there were footsteps to follow in. A path had been paved. Previous pioneers had lit the way. Here were people who did what I loved. They did it well. And they Looked. Like. Me. Here were people I could point to and shout to the world: 'See!? Look! **They** did it! So can I!' This wasn't a fantasy anymore. This was possible.

***

I'll tell you a secret. Being good at sport and physical activities takes work. A lot of work. For anyone. But dwarf and disabled people must work even harder than most. Often, we must work harder to produce the same results from our different, and often disadvantaged, bodies. As the proud owner of two strong short legs, I can tell you that I need to run **a lot** faster just to keep up with someone with longer legs. Similarly, shorter kids (and especially very short kids like me) with shorter arms need to push harder to propel a ball to a hoop that's further away from them than it is from taller kids.

But this isn't the hard part. Not really. The real challenge is how much harder we must work to defy what others think and expect of us, as disabled people. Let's say an average height, average weight, non-disabled child walks onto a football pitch or tennis court. People may look at them and give them the benefit of the doubt. They **could** be a decent footballer or tennis player. Even if, really, they've never kicked or hit a ball before. Now, if a visibly disabled person walks onto the same court, people may look at them and expect them to be less good than their average-height, non-disabled peers. Simply because of the way they look.

These are assumptions. They aren't based on evidence. On facts. That's why they're assumptions, see? But they are based on points of reference. On previous examples. Hear me out. If you see a million basketball players who all look like LeBron James, you might not imagine a basketball player could look like anyone else. It can be hard for dwarf and disabled kids to dream of being a champion swimmer if, until then, all the champion swimmers look like Michael Phelps. But, if a champion swimmer also looks like Ellie Simmonds – a dwarf and disabled woman and a former British Paralympian and World Champion swimmer – then, suddenly, everything seems so much more relatable. So much more reachable. Points of reference matter. A lot. That's why seeing heroes and role models who look like you – **whatever** you look like – is so very, very important.

So, I ask again. Who are your heroes? Do they look like you? I don't mean, do you wear a cape, a mask and are jacked with massive muscles (although, maybe you are, in which case, excellent work – all power to you). I mean, how far a stretch is it from their body to yours? Growing up, cool heroes with dwarfism weren't readily available to me. The Paralympics didn't get the attention it does now. Shows like *Game of Thrones* – which would make Peter Dinklage, a fantastic actor with dwarfism, a global star and household name – hadn't been made yet. Positive points of reference were very few and very far between.

There were plenty of horrible and demeaning points of reference, though. There were the Seven Dwarfs. Seven fictional dwarf men. Each so one dimensional they had names like 'Grumpy'. They were childish. Only one of them is remotely clever ('Doc', although I am in serious doubt of his medical credentials). Even that is me being generous. And they all live together in the woods, fawning over some weird, lost White lady. As an adult, I've lost count of the number of times a stranger has assumed – because of my body – that I am an actor in a nearby show of *Snow White*. Or made a joke if I say I feel 'sleepy'. Or shouted 'Heigh Ho' as I commit the crime of going about my own business.

Then there was the vile Mini-Me character from *Austin Powers*. He was like a biddable pet. He wasn't even his own person. He was a demeaning copy of an average height character. A small psychopathic doppelganger. Worse still, he was a target of ridicule and violence (which I promise you encourages real ridicule and real violence). Off-screen, the lives of several famous dwarf actors ended early. Tragically. As I said, cool dwarf heroes weren't always readily available. Instead, there were plenty of dwarf (and disabled and disfigured) characters who were either villains or objects of pity or the butts of jokes (and sometimes all three). Is it any wonder those two skateboarders were so precious to me?

But a change is in the wind. Finally, now, these days, people like Ellie Simmonds, Jahmani Swanson and Peter Dinklage are starting to get the respect, attention and acclaim they deserve. It's been a long time coming. And their successes don't make up for centuries of prejudice, discrimination and abuse. There is still much work to be done. Attitudes to change. Children to educate (and adults even more so). Stereotypes to smash. But I hope it is the beginning of a shift. A wonderful and irreversible shift.

I loved basketball. I loved skateboarding. Even if, in the end, I never went professional at either one. I loved these things, in and of themselves. The way they made me feel about myself. But here's the thing: the way I felt about myself was shaped by my ability to defy what **others** (and so much of society) assumed about me. Yes, I worked incredibly hard to defy people's expectations. But there was something even harder, something that I didn't do. And that is, to not have cared about those expectations in the first place. I don't say that lightly. I know how difficult that is – far, **far** harder than becoming the first dwarf marine or NBA championship winner.

Because those expectations, those assumptions, they're **everywhere**. All around us. They're spoken like they're facts. But they're not. They're judgements. Little drops of poison. So fine you barely notice them. But add them together. Drip. Drip. Drip. And together, these expectations, these assumptions, these judgements become something toxic. And they seep into everything. Almost unnoticed. Into the things we say. The words we speak. The things we watch. The books we read – including into this one. Into this very chapter. Did you notice?

Earlier in the story you're reading now, I said: 'I was a dwarf, sure, but I was decent on a deck.' A little droplet of venom right there, in that previous sentence. Read it again. Can you see it? It's the '**but**'. It took me years to learn to spot them. Phrases that start with: someone is disabled/neurodiverse/whatever. Then there's a 'but'. **Then** something positive about that person. For example: 'They're small **but** they're brave.' Or, 'They're disabled **but** they don't let that stop them.' These phrases are presented as positive. They're not. They're fake. What they really mean is that whatever comes before the 'but' is a **bad thing**. A bad thing for which that person must compensate – with the good thing that comes after. 'He had dwarfism, **but** he was a good skateboarder.' I'll add two more words just to make the hidden meaning crystal clear: 'He had dwarfism, **but at least** he was a good skateboarder.' You see it now, right? Now replace 'but' with 'and' and the meaning totally changes. 'He had dwarfism, **and** he was a good skateboarder.' There's no poison. My body is described, sure, and that may not be necessary – but it's not **judged**. There isn't a good or bad **value** placed on it. See the difference? I hope so. I wish I had when I was your age.

It's a lot. To love ourselves. Our bodies. To love them fearlessly. However beautifully different they may be. On their own imperfect terms. To not care what others think. I don't want to call that an act of heroism. Because, the truth is, it shouldn't have to be. We should all just be free to do so.

I wasn't always proud of my dwarfism. Not like I am now. It was especially hard when I was at school. I have scars, physical and mental, that I wish I didn't have. I am and always will be a work in progress. But dwarfism is the fire that burns inside me. It is part of my identity. It's who I am. It is in my bones and in my soul. Without it, I wouldn't have the biggest source of joy and love in my life – my little girls. They have dwarfism just like their mum. Just like me.

I hope that when they're older they can readily find people to look up to. People who look like them. Or who might have other disabilities and differences. Who help them to realise that, whatever their passions are – art, music, sport, anything they like – they can explore and enjoy and be valued for these on their own terms, as someone with dwarfism.

Who knows, maybe one day they'll even be asked to write their own list of heroes and role models. I'm pretty sure they'll have their own opinions about that. But, just in case they – or you – need a little inspiration, here are a few suggestions.

- Benjamin Lay – one of the first white radical abolitionists, Lay would carry out dramatic protests against the injustices of slavery. He always stood up for what he believed.
- Ellie Simmonds – a former British Paralympian and World Champion swimmer. She is a patron of the charity the Dwarf Sports Association UK. DSAuk works to make sport enjoyable and accessible to anyone and everyone with dwarfism in the UK.
- Peter Dinklage – a multiple award-winning actor and star of popular television series, *Game of Thrones*. He is also an animal rights advocate.
- Judy-Lynn del Rey – a leading publisher of popular sci-fi and fantasy books, she signed George Lucas's *Star Wars* a year before the movie was released.
- Jahmani Swanson – basketball player for the Harlem Globetrotters. Jahmani has travelled all around the world playing basketball.

He often talks about dwarfism to schoolchildren and offers to meet dwarf and disabled pupils.

- Sofiya Cheyenne – Sofiya is an actor, performance artist, public speaker, teacher, dancer and disability advocate. She has starred in many TV shows (including on Netflix and Amazon Prime) and theatre productions. Co-chair of the Dwarf Artist Coalition, many of her projects have showcased the power and ability of disabled people on stage, TV and film.

- Vilissa Thompson – disability rights consultant, social worker and writer. Vilissa helps others to challenge what they **think** they know about disability. She does this by teaching them to think about, for example, race and gender at the same time, and how each one affects and connects to the other (this is called 'intersectionality'). She has run social media campaigns like #DisabilityTooWhite. She also supports other disabled people to become their own advocates – within and outside of social work. Visit her website at: www.vilissathompson.com

- Mia Ives-Rublee – director for the Disability Justice Initiative at the Center for American Progress. She is a founder of the Women's March Disability Caucus (a group of people united to promote a cause). She helped to organise the original Women's March on Washington in 2017 – one of the most significant and impactful protests in years.
- And, of course, two skateboarders, called Pancho and Jason . . .

Ekinni Ìrìn Àjò Molẹbi – The First Family Adventure

by Matilda Feyiṣayọ Ibini

United Kingdon and Nigeria

Do you remember your last day of primary school or elementary school? Did you sign each other's shirts, take pictures, exchange tears, give your favourite teacher a thank-you card? I wish I could say that I remember my last day of primary school, except: I. Wasn't. There. No, I hadn't died – otherwise I wouldn't be able to tell you this story. But my mum had made a grave mistake when booking our flights for our first ever family holiday, from London, UK, to Lagos, Nigeria. (And no, the family trip to Brighton doesn't count because it was only for one day and we took a train.)

So, because my mum had made a mistake when booking our flights, instead of spending four weeks in Nigeria, we were going to spend six weeks there and miss the end of school term. Was this a trick, I wondered? Would we be coming back? Were we actually moving there? Because whenever Mum was upset at me and my siblings, she always threatened to send us to Nigeria.

'**Ma binu oko mi** – don't be upset, darling,' she said in Yorùbá. But I **was** upset, I was going to miss the farewell assembly, miss signing each other's shirts, taking pictures and properly saying goodbye to the best primary school friends in the world. Nothing my mum said was going to make the heaviness in my stomach lighter.

'I'm going to make sure you and your siblings enjoy this trip even more,' Mum smiled.

I made a deal with my mum: because I was missing the last week of school, I wouldn't have to do my physio stretches on holiday. That was the only time I've ever gotten out of doing them. I absolutely hated physiotherapy! It was painful and made me feel bad about all the things I couldn't do. So, that was something, at least. But she did make me pack my leg splints, the ones I had to wear for an hour a day. I thought to myself: **what if I just forget to wear them? I already have to wear adapted shoes, isn't that enough?**

***

In the run-up to this first ever family holiday, most Saturdays were spent with our mum, buying suitcases, food and drinks we liked.

311

'Don't they have Capri-Sun in Nigeria?' my younger sister asked, as our mum put several boxes into the trolley.

'Not the kind you like,' she replied.

My little brother sat in the children's seat of the trolley, kicking his feet.

'You excited to meet Grandma in Nigeria?' Mum asked as she stroked his giggling face.

I don't know if I could say I was excited – curious, maybe. I had a feeling that the problems I faced in London would follow me. They often did. It didn't matter if I was staying overnight at my godmother's house, or if I was on a school trip: my body would find one way or another to betray me. You see, if you'd met me and I was sitting down, I could almost pass for a non-disabled child. But from the moment I stood up, the cloak disappeared (instead of me – which I'd often wish). I walked with a very obvious limp. Some people described the way I walked as like the Hunchback of Notre Dame. Those people were not people I would call friends. I thought I walked somewhere in between a ballerina and the cartoon character Goofy. Actually, now that I think about it, I walked like both: a Goofy ballerina. Yep, that's me! **Ah-hyuck**! I always preferred him over Mickey Mouse anyway.

People often asked my mum, 'What's wrong with her? Why does she walk like that? If she doesn't stop, she could get stuck like that!' If they asked me, my answer would always be the same: 'I have a medical condition.' And, if you were to ask me what that meant, I would shrug my shoulders before any words got a chance to form in my mouth. It's just what my mum told me to tell people, partly because we didn't know the name of my disability until I was a teenager.

The symptoms started when I was five: I began walking on my toes (yes, like a ballerina, my heels lifting off the ground). It's like the muscles had turned to concrete, and no physiotherapist or masseuse could get my heels to touch the ground again, no matter how hard they tried. Even though I had yearly tests to rule things out, it never felt like we were getting any closer to answers, and we wouldn't get confirmation of my medical condition until I was thirteen (two years after our trip to Nigeria): 'She has limb-girdle muscular dystrophy – LGMD,' they'd say.

When I was told that, I didn't understand what that meant either, but it is one of the few memories I have of seeing my mum cry. LGMD affects the muscles in your shoulders and hips, aka the girdle muscles, and so as a result I'd always struggled to walk and carry things in my arms. One of the main symptoms was falling to the ground and not being able to get up without assistance because my arms were too weak. By some miracle, despite my hundreds of falls, I've never broken a bone (yet). As a child I would fall at home, up the stairs, down the stairs, at school, church, supermarkets, cinemas, leisure centres, hospitals, off kerbs, off the bus, on the bus, out of cars, taxis and (to get back to the story in hand) at the airport. Heathrow, to be precise.

At Heathrow airport, on our way to Nigeria, my mum and older sister helped me up after a fall, and my knee was vibrating. So, the friendly staff at Heathrow offered to transport me and my family in their electric carts through the airport and right up to our gate. Sadly, they didn't let me drive the cart. I never imagined how big an airport could be, and my legs had already buckled before we'd begun the journey to our plane.

We were heading to the terminal, taking off from Heathrow and landing at Murtala Muhammed International Airport, Lagos. As we zoomed through the airport, my knee began to vibrate less, and instead it just felt really sore. I wondered if we would have made our flight if I had walked all the way. We were on that cart for so long that it felt as though we must have reached Lagos itself. We disembarked the cart and joined a long queue of people: aunties and uncles dressed like they were going to a party, families with young children, elderly people, all waiting to board the plane. There were a few steps to climb but, supported by my mum and older sister, it wasn't long until we were physically on the plane, and I finally sat down, with my knee throbbing once more.

Hours later, seat belts buckled tightly, the plane landed to a symphony of cries and tears from the young children (my little brother included), whose ears painfully popped. I can't lie, I would have cried too if I'd felt brave enough. Coming back, our mum made sure we packed earplugs.

As soon as the plane doors opened, a type of heat hit my body in a way I'd never felt before. In London, I had never felt this type of intense heat. By the time we made it to collect our luggage, I was sweating so much I had to tie my jacket around my waist. Thankfully, Murtala Muhammed International Airport, Lagos, was a much smaller airport, so I could walk all the way through.

Once we had reached the last checks, the smiling airport staff asked my mum: 'So, what have you got for us, Ma?' He raised his eyebrows to his colleagues like they were in on some joke. My mum sighed before reaching into her bag, taking out a few notes.

'Hope you and the kids enjoy your stay, Ma.' He palmed the cash from her.

I tugged at my mum's top. 'Why did you give that man money?'

She gave me a look that told me, **I'll explain later**. And with our many, many bags, we exited the airport into Lagos. It was night-time, sometime after 9 p.m. An old woman walked over slowly. She smiled at me. I smiled nervously back; she looked familiar but I was sure I'd never met her.

'**Ma'mi**!' my mum said as she rushed over to her, and they embraced. They held each other tight. My mum wiped tears from her mum's face.

'Come and meet your grandma.'

'Who's Grandma?' my younger brother genuinely asked.

'Ah-ah. You've spoken to Grandma over the phone before. This is my mum,' she chuckled.

'You have a mum?' my younger sister piped up. 'Then how old is Grandma?'

I flicked my little sister's ear. I don't even know how old our mum is and I also know not to ask. Adults don't like it when you ask them how old they are. I think it's because they can't remember.

Our grandma cupped each of our faces as she smiled, laughed and cried all at the same time. 'Fey-Fey!' she hugged me tight. I almost lost my balance. I'd not been in Lagos a day and I already had a nickname – one that I actually liked for once. She then helped me push my trolley, as we all made our way to the taxi rank.

In the taxi to our grandma's house, we got to see Lagos at night, and it was much livelier than London. So many people were out, there weren't many streetlights, lots of traffic illuminated the area. The pavements were thin, so most people looked like shadows, appearing then disappearing around cars.

Our grandma lived in Ifako Agege, in a baby-blue bungalow, with a tin-sheet roof, a veranda and a massive compound in front. This was the first time I'd stayed in a home that didn't have stairs. The only time buildings didn't have stairs were in the stories I wrote, but I'd never imagined it possible in the real world. All this time my grandma had been living in a house I needed. I wished we could pick up the house and bring it back with us. The taxi parked up in front of two large gates and beeped its horn a few times, alerting someone to open the gates so the taxi could drive into the compound. As the driver helped get the luggage out of the boot, my mum helped lift me to my feet. Most cars, chairs, toilets are too low for me to get up from on my own, and my arms are too weak to support me, so my mum and older sister lifted me any time I couldn't myself.

'**Se o wa dada?** – Is she OK?' the driver asked as he slammed the boot shut.

'**Ese ndun** – Her leg is hurting,' my mum replied.

'**Se ofe iranlowo?** – Do you want help?'

'**Rara. Ese.** – No, thank you.'

It's funny because my mum's reply to anyone Yorùbá who asks about me is '**Ese ndun**', which translates to 'their legs hurt or are paining them', which both is and isn't true. My legs do hurt sometimes but that phrase suggests my legs hurt all the time, which is to suggest the pain in my legs is permanent. And when my legs hurt, it forces me to walk differently or stops me from being able to do things myself. It's funny how language works. Like, I can't speak Yorùbá. I can speak a little when I'm mimicking Mum but I understand everything she says in Yorùbá, everything her friends say, everything they say in Nollywood films, well most of what they say and the lyrics to fújì music. But I can't speak it. When my mum speaks to me in Yorùbá, I answer in English.

***

When we entered Grandma's house, the first things she switched on were the ceiling fans. She had one in every room. I felt a great relief for the breeze – a warm one, but a breeze all the same. Grandma had made rice and stew for us to eat, which we happily ate around midnight. This was probably the latest I'd stayed up. I could get used to this.

And then, just as we were finally getting ready for bed, the lights went out. Me and my siblings screamed, while our grandma and mum laughed.

'**Nepa ti muna lo** – NEPA has taken the electricity.'

We soon learned that NEPA (the National Electric Power Authority) switched off electricity whenever they liked, even when you paid your bills. It was very annoying but you either bought a generator or just got used to candlelight. In the six weeks we'd be staying with Grandma, it wouldn't be the first or the last time this happened – I lost count after the tenth time.

This trip had many more adventures in store. On our first day in Lagos, we had so many visitors. Two of my mum's brothers and their families. Cousins we'd never met before. Mum's school friends, childhood friends, all visited with their families, to come and marvel at the group of UK kids who couldn't speak a word of Yorùbá, but definitely understood everything that was being said – especially when they made jokes about our accent, clothes and occasionally the way I walked. But none of that mattered. We were in Lagos, and so we did as Lagosians did. We came to **chop**! – to eat good food.

When it came to food, we were spoiled for choice. If it wasn't the fresh hot breakfasts our grandma made us every morning – the family favourite being yam and egg – Nigeria had its own fast food and chain restaurants, and we ate in as many as we could: Mr Biggs, Sweet Sensation, Tantalizers. And if that wasn't enough, there wasn't a day where you wouldn't come across street hawkers selling: 'Pure water, pure water!', 'Fresh Agege bread, fresh Agege bread!', '**O lo oge ti de o** – the oge seller is here!', 'Gala. Gala. Get your Gala!'

Whenever we were in a taxi, we could buy snacks like **chin chin**, **akara** and plantain crisps while we sat in traffic. It was like the whole nation wanted everyone to eat well. It was like we were on tour. We were out almost every day, so my nervousness about how I walked, and how I'd fall over, quickly disappeared – I was distracted by the new places and people we were visiting. We stayed with relatives and family friends in their homes in Surulere, Ajangbadi, Ketu, Ilorin, Aguda, Victoria Island and Lekki. We went to Badagry Beach and Bar Beach and I fell because it's hard for me to walk on uneven surfaces, but it didn't matter because the sand was warm, the sea was endless and most beaches sold delicious **suya** and Nigerian Fanta, and you could take a horse ride.

My mum let my siblings get on the horse but not me. It's frustrating sometimes, because my mum treats me like I'm made of glass. And not just any glass but like the kind that is so fragile that if you looked at it wrong, it would crack. She also didn't let me ride an **okada** (motorbike) – that one stung a bit more because even my grandma used them almost weekly to get around. My old grandma could get on motorbikes but I couldn't.

I tried to not let it stop all the other things I enjoyed about the trip. We got to see all these different sides to Nigeria. Nigerian public transport at the bus depot reminded me of what it's like being in Piccadilly Circus, lots of people and yellow buses, called **danfo**, in every direction you turned. Bus drivers yelling out the stops they're going to, to fill up their buses before they go. We piled in, all six of us, and somehow they managed to fit ten more people on a bus that should only seat about eight, including the driver. Thankfully my knee was feeling much better by this point; my grandma had given it quite a strong massage with Aboniki Balm every day since we arrived. The pain in my knee was no match for the heat from the Aboniki Balm and Lagos weather. The motorways were surrounded by endless and dense forests. The bush, Grandma told us, was filled with magical creatures and you must never venture through them at night otherwise you will never find your way out. I knew she was telling the truth – I'd watched far too many Nollywood films for it not to be.

Nigeria was also big on recycling – most drinks were sold or served in glass bottles and there were so many places that accepted them back once you'd finished. One of my favourite places was visiting my grandma's stall in Better

Life Market in Ogba. She sold spices and foodstuffs and she was very popular. It was like we were with a celebrity when we visited her at her market stall. She was one of the founders of Better Life Market, so everyone called her 'Mama Betterlife'.

One day, we went to a friend-of-a-friend's birthday party that was overrun with bush rats, so we left. **Alangba** (lizards) and bush rats ran the streets the same way foxes run London streets – they were everywhere, and they didn't care who saw them. One even chased my sister into Grandma's house and it took a whole day of moving furniture to show it the exit.

Grandma taught us how to play Ludo. We visited Nigeria's National Museum. We went to the **Eyo** festival, and it is no Lord Mayor's show – it's better! Adults and children dressed up as masqueraders in white flowing robes that covered them from head to toe, including their faces, because they represented the spirits of the ancestors. The **Eyo** wore different coloured, broad-brimmed hats that looked like sombreros, while holding decorated wooden staffs. The colour of these hats were red, blue, green and purple, and each hat had a distinct shield which represented the Royal Palace the **Eyo** was from. We must have seen hundreds of masqueraders dancing, jumping and singing during the procession that lead them to the shrine of the **Orisa** (deity) **Eyo**. When an **Eyo** turns their attention to you, out of respect you must bow your head. It was both thrilling and a little scary. One of them came too close to my younger brother and sister, who ran screaming and hid behind Mum and my older sister.

We went for walks in parks and stayed up late, especially when NEPA took the electricity for the umpteenth time. It wasn't long before I needed a few days' rest to recover from all our day trips and overnight stays. My siblings would go out for a few hours with relatives and I would stay and help Grandma make dinner for when they returned. It felt different being in my body, something about being in constant warm weather quietened a lot of the growling aches and pains I'd normally feel daily in London. It's like my body sighed contently any time I sat on the veranda with a cold drink that wouldn't stay cold for long.

***

But despite the busy days out, seeing new places and meeting new people, I couldn't ignore the elephant in the room: the homeless population and how most of the people begging on the streets walked like I did. Had limbs shaped like mine. But they didn't have wheelchairs or crutches – instead they used other objects to help them move, such as skateboards and wheelbarrows. **Is this how I would have been treated if I had been born in Nigeria?** I wondered. Mum and Grandma left my siblings at our cousins', and took me to a church to meet with a pastor for special prayers. I wondered if this pastor had prayed for the disabled people in their country, and why (if those prayers hadn't been answered) my mum's or grandma's would be.

Grandma and Mum gave an offering to the pastor. Miracles are just as expensive in Nigeria as they are in London. As the pastor and his anointed crew began shouting to the heavens for my miracle to be delivered, I didn't feel closer to God. I felt embarrassed. I felt alone, even with all these people around me. I wanted to shrink into myself. I wanted to disappear. I'd always had a complicated relationship with Christianity but this trip had definitely lessened my faith. I didn't tell my mum that, though, I just said 'amen'.

No one chooses where they are born, not even the body they are born into, but, if anything, you just have to make the best of what you have. Despite the list of things I couldn't do constantly growing, I tried my best to focus on the things I could do – because they did exist, even if that list was much shorter. Like, I'd never imagined I'd be on the other side of the world when most of the time in London I couldn't get into a shop if it had too many stairs, or I'd avoid going out because I'd get tired really quickly – but there was something about Nigeria where I welcomed these challenges. Perhaps because travelling was new to me, and it's exciting going to places you haven't been to before.

Nigeria was just as hard to navigate as London but people were different there and it felt OK that I was different too. There was a can-do attitude to everything I encountered, whereas in London, I was more used to just walking away and not bothering. And it helped that the weather was very welcoming. I still got tired but this time it was earned. I was tired because I was having fun and going on surprising adventures. Nigeria wasn't perfect, just like London wasn't perfect, but at least during this holiday I'd not been made to feel like a problem, as I often felt back home. I just got to be me.

***

By the time we got back to Grandma's it was dark and my siblings still weren't back yet. I sat on a chair on the veranda and looked up. It wasn't the first time that I'd seen stars before, but this was . . . this was incredible. My eyes couldn't see them all at once, there were too many. I couldn't stop looking up – it was like I was having a staring competition that I didn't want to lose. I could look up, counting them forever. There's something about seeing so many stars, and feeling really small, my fears feeling small, my problems feeling small. I'd always loved learning about space and stars, because once I found out that there was no gravity in space, I would often dream about a world I could float through – never having to fall, or struggle to climb a step ever again.

'You don't see stars like this in London, **abi**?' my mum put her arm around me while we stargazed on Grandma's veranda. Then a lizard ran towards us. I screamed and we rushed inside laughing and catching our breath.

Six weeks in Lagos and I didn't want to leave. My body was used to this heat now, my muscles didn't feel as tense or painful. There was a different pace in Nigeria, one that could feel both exciting and overwhelming. But most of all, I knew when we left I was going to miss my grandma, her step-free bungalow, the food and our shared jokes. There would be tears at the airport from us all. I would give anything to rewind those six weeks.

When we came back to London, it seemed different, or maybe I was a little different. As I lay in bed back in my bedroom, the next day being my first day of secondary school, I knew I'd faced everything in Nigeria. Now, it felt like there was nothing I couldn't do. **Secondary school**, I thought – **I'm ready for you**.

Pomegranate

by Elle McNicoll

United Kingdom

'Have you got your dress yet?'

I was asked the question in English. We had all been reading a terrible book about the Titanic. It was an ancient school novel; I could tell because it had clearly been read by about thirty people before me. I didn't understand how anyone could take one of the most tragic and yet fascinating accidents in human history and make it dull.

My mind tried to wander back to the question. It was asked by Amy, who had turned around in her chair to address me while Mrs Durham left the classroom with one of the hockey girls, in order to scold her in private.

'Have. You,' Amy spoke again in a patronisingly slow manner, 'Got. Your. Dress. Yet?'

Everyone in school always spoke to me like that. They rolled their eyes, they spoke slowly, they would laugh with each other and cast nasty, scathing looks over at me. I had learned to bear it and, perhaps, somewhere deep inside, I believed that they were right to do it. I struggled socially; my handwriting had alerted the teachers to some mysterious neurodevelopmental disability that I didn't even understand. Within a few months of starting at this fancy new school, they had begun carting me off to Special Educational Needs classes.

Whenever I was removed from my regular classroom, I could feel the other girls watching me with hungry derision.

I might as well have worn a sash with the letter A for Autistic written on it. I felt branded. I was wearing a label I didn't understand and I didn't know how to fit into it.

'She's so weird,' Meghan whispered to Harriet and Amy, who snorted. She made sure it was loud enough for me to hear. 'Probably doesn't own a dress.'

'Do you know what a dress is?' Amy asked, pretending to sound concerned and caring when her eyes were dancing with glee and cruelty.

'I haven't got a dress yet,' was all I was able to mumble.

The Dance was scheduled for June. I had already walked out of one school disco because the lights flashed too much and the music was terrible. I'd gone home, and hadn't told anyone, and it wasn't until the following Monday that I realised there had been some mass hysteria about my exit. One of the boys started a rumour saying I'd climbed onto the back of someone's motorbike. These rumours had spread like lit powder, and it was horrifying to realise that my want for invisibility had led to me being perceived and discussed in such an intense way.

This upcoming dance was a ball. So much more than a disco. There were eyes on all of us. The boys from the boys' school would be there, and the night's theme was 'Heroes and Villains'.

'Do you think you'll be able to make it through this time around?' Amy asked, and some of her friends smirked.

'Can she even afford a dress?' Harriet whispered, not quietly enough for me to miss it.

My pencil snapped against my exercise book but I didn't look up at any of them. School was just prison time. It was a sentence placed on me and I had to just get through it. Eventually, the cell door would be unlocked and I would be allowed to walk free. There was no time off for good behaviour, but rising to people's attempts to goad me would only prolong my incarceration.

And the neurodivergent schoolkids always face harsher punishments and are watched with more suspicion. It's never said in so many words but I felt it. When I was removed from lessons, I felt it. It told the others: she's different. Have at her. Make her feel it. Make her remember it.

When Mrs Durham and the red-faced girl she had been scolding returned to the English classroom, quiet reading returned. I pushed the Titanic book to one side and surreptitiously slid out my scrapbook. It was a heavy hardback thing I'd bought in the Jenners sale. It was full of beautiful dresses and colourful art that I had printed off from my mum's office computer or cut out of magazines. I would trawl the internet for stunning outfits and eccentric people. I would stick them between the pages until the book grew to twice its size.

The future will look like this, I would tell myself. This is the sepia part of life. The colour is coming.

New York skyscrapers and London landmarks. Vivienne Westwood. Manolo Blahnik. Stephen Sondheim.

Howard Ashman. Nora Ephron. They were all between the pages. Quotes from Charles Dickens, Taylor Swift and Tony Kushner.

I was getting out. I didn't mind being grey and unnoticed in the meantime.

I ate lunch by myself and then sat by the lockers in our form room. Rosie, Hilary and Becca all talked about boys and gossiped while I stared at the clock on the wall. Rosie would occasionally glance over at me with a quizzical look. She was my favourite of my fellow inmates. Intelligent, charismatic, witty, vibrant and fun.

I knew she was waiting to escape, too. Though we never spoke of such things. We never did. Serious matters were never topics of conversation.

Tom Waits was singing into one of my ears, as I only wore one headphone.

'Who are you going to be for the dance?' Rosie eventually asked me.

I knew she probably wouldn't go. She had loads of friends from her old school, and from her neighbourhood, and they had parties on Fridays that were much more exciting than a silly school costume ball.

I decided to skip PE and go to the library. If anyone noticed I was missing, I'd say I was with Matron or attending a last-minute counselling session. The upside to being considered the Weird Kid is having multiple possible alibis.

The only fond memory I would hold close from my senior school days would be the library.

The quiet, the calm and the soft colours were comforting enough. But the greatest virtue of the library was the reminder that the shelves were full of other people who had also made it out. Their escapes were defiantly locked into their stories. I knew instinctively through reading novels that the authors had overcome places just like my prison.

I heard someone say my name. Now, my old name. A name I no longer use as it was never truly mine. It was a name for another girl, not the girl I wanted to be. Not the one I am now. It was for someone meek and timid and well-behaved. It was for someone who would give their pencil to another student and never ask for it back. Who would let people push her in the corridor. Who would speak softly and have no courage in what she was saying.

It was that girl's name. And I wasn't her. Not anymore.

I stood up, as we were made to do when teachers addressed us.

It was Miss Brydon, my old head of year. She was the one I had been made to write my apology letter to after leaving the school disco without telling anybody I was going home.

'We're not going to have any silliness at next week's dance, are we?'

It was both a question and a command.

'No,' I said in a monotone voice, my gaze fixed to her forehead instead of her eyes. 'No silliness.'

'Good. I know things might get overwhelming for you sometimes, but you're a big girl now. You know how to behave.'

Behave. I know how they behave. I've watched them all my life. I've learned to copy, to mimic, in order to pass as one of them.

'Yes.'

'And there are lots of children like you, with special needs, and they have much bigger problems.'

338

She doesn't see my fist clench and unclench at her use of 'special needs'.

'Do you know which character you're going to be?' she asked, aiming for friendliness.

'No,' I said, truthfully. 'It's easier for the boys.'

Heroes and Villains. For every one female character, there were ten male. I could have easily dressed as a male hero or villain but I would never have been able to live it down among the other girls, who already found me strange.

'Well, there's Wonder Woman,' Miss Brydon said unhelpfully.

Nowadays, a dance of Heroes and Villains would have been more enjoyable. The Golden Age of Marvel Comics, and a million new television shows and books, had yet to arrive. This was before Katniss Everdeen.

This was before so many things.

The sound of my old, unwanted name jolted me out of my train of thought once more. Harriet, Meghan and Amy were watching from the computer lab. Harriet made a concerted effort to whisper something nasty to her two friends from behind her hands and they all looked over at me before breaking into loud, obnoxious laughter.

I felt small. Nervous. I wanted to hide. I had tried so hard, for so many years, to be invisible. To avoid other people's jeers and whispers. I had been so open and sweet upon arriving at this school. I had wanted to be everyone's friend.

That girl was lost to me now.

'Just keep up the good attendance,' Miss Brydon said.

***

As I ate dinner, I thought about names. I thought about the heavily male world of heroes and villains. The binary of it all. The black and white view. Maybe goodness was a spectrum, because most days I felt a mixture of both hero and villain. I would start the day with the intention of being good and a million things would derail me.

I had no comic books in my room but I did have mythology. Hardback books, mostly presents from friends of the family, and they were all about Greek and Roman myths. I was fascinated by the Romans effectively renaming all of the Greek gods to create their own narrative. Aphrodite became Venus. Aries became

Mars. Eros to Cupid, Hermes to Mercury.

I turned one page, to a spread about a goddess in pale pink and blue. Who wore flowers in her long hair. I stared at the illustration for the longest time. She was tall, like me. She had long gold hair, like me. There was a touch of anger in her.

I felt more than a touch of anger in me.

When I ordered the costume online, Dad stood over my shoulder with his debit card. He stared at the long white dress with the golden belt.

'I don't know this story,' he said casually. He was probably just relieved to see me mildly interested in doing something social. 'Won't other people be dressed as superheroes?'

'Probably,' I allowed, clicking **Order**.

'But you want to be . . . this?'

'Yes.'

'Okay.'

He was unsure of how to talk to me. It was just the two of us in the house now and I could feel him always walking on eggshells around me. Not because we

had a bad relationship, or because we were prone
to arguing.

I think he could sense I was fragile. Like a vase that
was missing a tiny fleck of clay. It looked like all of the
other pieces of pottery but people whispered about it
being made wrong. Missing something that the others
all had.

But I had made myself whole. I did so with stories.

The Japanese paint the cracks in their pottery with gold,
highlighting the alleged flaws and making them more
beautiful.

I could do that. I could take this label the doctors had
given me, and the names the playground had thrown at
me, and I could paint gold into the cracks.

***

The costume arrived. It fitted like a glove. I tied the
golden sash around my waist and admired the slit
on the side of the long white dress. I sat before my
bedroom mirror and emptied a Boots carrier bag onto
the floorboards. I covered up one small blackhead on
my nose with the concealer. I played with some powder.
I laced mascara through my lashes. Then gold. Lots of
gold. I lathered my eyelids with golden dust, the more

I could get on the brush the better. A second coat. A third.

I stared at my reflection. I looked so different. As if someone new was lurking behind my eyes, waiting to come out.

Persephone. Goddess of spring. Queen of the Underworld. Not a traditional superhero. Not exactly a villain. Something grey and complex in between.

As my dad pulled up to the school, the hall already pulsing with music and packed with fellow students, he turned off the engine and glanced at me.

'If it all gets too much,' he said quietly, 'just let a teacher know this time. And they'll phone me.'

I stared ahead at the school. 'I'll be fine.'

And yet, I couldn't open the car door just yet.

'I know they aren't nice to you,' Dad added. He didn't sound guilty. Just resigned. 'I know it's hard.'

It's difficult to breathe into words how hard it really is. Being part of a small club of humans who are just, for some reason, made different. The thousands of cuts are as important as the big swings.

'I'll be fine,' I repeated.

I got out of the car. I walked in golden sandals, with golden dust on my eyes, towards the entrance. With each step, I promised myself I would be gone someday. One day, this place will not be the everyday. It will not take up the majority of my life or my thoughts or my waking hours. I will be free of it. Everyone else will sign yearbooks and wail and weep, and I will already be gone.

The long white dress swept the concrete ground as I walked towards the glass doors. Two teachers sat behind a desk at the entrance and they stared in astonishment at me.

'Who's this then, I'm drawing a blank?' Dr Hely said to Miss Leslie. The latter shook her head in confusion.

Both of them had taught me for a couple of years.

'Elle,' I said, testing out the new name, the real name, on my tongue like a drop of spice after too much dryness. 'Elle McNicoll.'

The one you rolled your eyes at, I wanted to say. The one you tutted at. The one you let the other kids push around right in front of you.

I walked inside. My spine was straight. My shoulders

were back. My face was fixed, stony and strong. No longer scanning people's faces for approval.

Great fashion can do that for you. It can become an armour. The arrows fired at you are exactly the same, but you can deflect them. They bounce off your chain mail. They can't hurt you anymore.

Stories had been my salvation in difficult schooldays. I told myself about the future. Escaping school. I told myself that the label wouldn't be misunderstood forever. Someday, somehow, it would get easier. The little girl who had tried to befriend everyone, she was still in me. Locked safely in a small pocket of air between my ribs. She would come out when it was safe.

In the meantime, there was Elle. She wasn't scared of bullies. She didn't hide in the toilets. She dressed as the Queen of the Underworld and wore golden eyeshadow. She looked people in the eye and never smiled.

As I entered the room, people stepped aside. They parted automatically, as if there was some kind of spell commanding it. They stared open-mouthed, unsure of what to do or say. There were so many Batmans, Spider-Mans and Wonder Womans. A few Supergirls. One Catwoman.

They gaped at Persephone in confusion. I felt people's eyes like a spotlight and it no longer concerned me. I was mad with newness. I wasn't going to be their pet or their sport or their punching bag anymore. I wasn't going to be the butt of the joke. I wouldn't avert my gaze, shuffle on by or try to appease people.

I was not going to make myself smaller to allow them to feel bigger.

I would rather have a disability than be like them. The realisation hit me as I stood in the middle of the dance floor, while everyone stared and the music pounded.

I would rather be like this. I would rather this than have their smallness. Their cowardice.

They would always be here. In this room. It would never get bigger or better for them.

I would fly higher. And my whole life would be 'who does she think she is?', and 'how dare she?', and 'what arrogance!'. I would like myself so much, it would seem like defiance to the neurotypicals.

And I would bring other people with me.

Harriet, Meghan and Amy staggered to the front of the crowd and Amy looked me up and down. But, for the first time, it wasn't in a nasty way. It was in disbelief and bewilderment.

'Who are you meant to be?' she asked, dressed as Batgirl and looking so young and so silly.

I closed my eyes and let the electricity of my different brain send sparks all the way through me. It felt like the power of a god, too difficult to contain and bind. It needed to break free.

Me. I'm meant to be me. It's been so long. Too long. But it's time.

About the Contributors

Jen Campbell is an award-winning poet, and the bestselling author of fourteen books for adults and children, spanning fiction, non-fiction, poetry and picture books. Her titles include the Franklin and Luna series, *The Sister Who Ate Her Brothers* and *The Beginning of the World in the Middle of the Night*. Her books have been translated into more than twenty languages. She is also an editor and a disability advocate, and she reviews books online, in print and on the radio. You can find her talking about reading, the history of fairy tales, and disability over on her YouTube channel, where she has a following of over 70,000. www.jen-campbell.co.uk

James Catchpole runs a children's literary agency with his wife Lucy in Oxford, England. He sometimes writes about a child-version of himself called Joe, as in the award-winning picture books *What Happened to You?* and *You're So Amazing!*. He filled some of the time between being Joe's age and the age he is now as an amputee footballer and itinerant busker, two professions where it actively helps to have one leg.

Lucy Catchpole is the author of *Mama Car* and co-author of *You're So Amazing!*. She's a full-time wheelchair user and has written about disability for the *Guardian* and the BBC, and more often on her Instagram @thecatchpoles, where she and James also post about children's books and family life with their two daughters.

Sophie Kamlish is an illustrator, animator and three-time Paralympic athlete based in Bath, England. She graduated from Kingston University in 2019 with a degree in illustration and animation and has illustrated for the BBC and animated for both Channel 4 and the Royal Opera House. In 2019, her final-year animation, in which she discusses the pros and cons of life as an amputee, was nominated for the London International Animation Festival. Sophie ran the 100m for Great Britain at the London 2012 Paralympics when she was just sixteen. Life as an athlete has taken her all over the world – her pencil case firmly packed alongside her prosthetic running blade.

Ali Abbas grew up on his family farm in Baghdad. He came to public attention as a child in 2003, when at the outset of the Iraq war he and his family were bombed. The *New Yorker* magazine published a photo of him that became iconic of the impact of the war on innocent civilians. Newly disabled, he became a British citizen, studying at Hall School in Wimbledon alongside his friend Ahmed. He has a son, and lives in South London.

Polly Atkin (FRSL) is a poet and non-fiction writer. Her two poetry collections are *Basic Nest Architecture* and *Much With Body*. Her non-fiction books are *Recovering Dorothy: The Hidden Life of Dorothy Wordsworth*, *Some Of Us Just Fall: On Nature and Not Getting Better* and *The Company of Owls*, all of which deal with the natural world and disabled lives in different ways. She works as a freelancer from her home in the English Lake District, where she co-owns historic Grasmere bookshop Sam Read Bookseller. www.pollyatkin.com

Imani Barbarin is an American writer, public speaker, actor and disability rights advocate. With a following of over a million on social media, she posts as @crutchesandspice on TikTok and Instagram, and is the creator of viral hashtags like #AbledsAreWeird and #ThingsDisabledPeopleKnow on X. Writing as a Black disabled woman, her finely observed commentary often explores the complex intersection between race and disability. Her first book – a memoir titled *If I Were You,*

I'd Kill Myself – will be published in 2026. Imani studied creative writing at Eastern University, French at the Sorbonne and has a master's in global communications from the American University of Paris.

Christa Couture is an award-winning performing and recording artist, non-fiction writer, filmmaker and broadcaster. Host of the Canadian TV travel show *Postcards From*, she is proudly Indigenous (mixed Cree and Scandinavian), queer and disabled. Her maternity photos – heavily pregnant and wearing her iconic floral prosthetic leg – went viral, picked up by websites and newspapers across the world. Her memoir *How To Lose Everything* was published in 2020.

Carly Findlay (OAM) is an award-winning writer, speaker, arts worker and appearance activist. Her first book, a memoir called *Say Hello*, was released in January 2019. Carly edited the anthology *Growing Up Disabled in Australia* and she writes on disability and appearance diversity issues for news outlets including the CNN, ABC, *The Age* and *Sydney Morning Herald* and SBS. She works part-time at Melbourne Fringe helping artists make their work accessible and working closely with Deaf and disabled artists. In 2020, she received a Medal of the

Order of Australia (OAM) for her work as a disability advocate and activist. www.carlyfindlay.com.au

Dr M. Leona Godin is the author of *There Plant Eyes: A Personal and Cultural History of Blindness* and the founder of Aromatica Poetica, an arts and culture laboratory for the advancement of smell and taste. Her writing has appeared in such venues as the *New York Times*, Literary Hub and *ARTnews*. Leona has a PhD in English literature, and lectures on multisensory and multimodal approaches to art and accessibility. She also creates scented/tactile performance journeys that explore the rich potentials of sensory translation and disability aesthetics. She lives with her partner in the lively Lower East Side of New York City.

Eugene Grant is a writer and activist interested in media representation and the history of disability and dwarfism. He's written for the *Guardian*, *Independent* and the *New Statesman*. Eugene contributed to *Disability Visibility* with his chapter 'The Fearless Benjamin Lay: Activist, Abolitionist, Dwarf Person', and *Body Talk* with 'The Body That Betrayed Me'. In both 2018 and 2019 he was named one of the Disability Power 100 by the Shaw Trust.

Jan Grue is a Norwegian writer, academic and actor. He is the author of a novel, children's books and several collections of short stories. His memoir *I Live a Life Like Yours* won the Norwegian Critics Prize for Literature, and became the first Norwegian non-fiction book nominated for the Nordic Council Literature Prize in fifty years. As an actor, he appeared in the Norwegian political thriller series *Occupied* and reflected on his experience in the *Guardian*, writing about the long entanglement of disability and villainy in fiction. Jan is Professor of Sociology at the University of Oslo, and lives in Oslo with his wife and son.

Matilda Feyişayọ Ibini is a Nigerian-Londoner, a multi-award-winning bionic, playwright, author and filmmaker. Matilda has limb girdle muscular dystrophy and is a wheelchair user. They were a Star of Tomorrow 2020; a feature screenplay they co-wrote was selected as part of The Brit List; and they were a BFI Flare x BAFTA 2023 mentee. They have written audio dramas for BBC Radio 3, BBC Radio 4 and Audible, and their last play, *Sleepova*, won them the Most Promising Playwright Award at the 2023 Critics' Circle Theatre Awards, and the 2024 Olivier Award for Outstanding Achievement in Affiliate Theatre. www.matildaibini.com

Ilya Kaminsky is a hard-of-hearing, USSR-born, Ukrainian-Russian-Jewish-American poet, critic, translator and professor. He is best known for his books *Dancing in Odessa* and *Deaf Republic*, which won the Whiting Writer's Award, the American Academy of Arts and Letters' Metcalf Award, and numerous others. He co-founded Poets For Peace, an organisation which sponsors poetry readings in the United States and abroad with a goal of supporting such relief organisations as Doctors Without Borders and Survivors International. In 2019, the BBC named Kaminsky among '12 Artists who changed the world'.

Sora J. Kasuga (any/all) is a writer, speaker, professional circus artist and model, the founder of The FaceOut Project, and co-founder of CirqOvation. Proudly Japanese-American, disabled/facially different, neurodivergent and queer, Kasuga's many identities fuel their work to shift individual and collective perceptions in order to create a more inclusive, equitable and just world. In a society built on shutting certain people out, Sora reaches for an inclusive humanity that emerges stronger because of our differences, not despite them. Their latest endeavour is The FaceOut Project, promoting community and activism around facial difference. www.faceoutproject.com

Jessica Kellgren-Fozard is a British YouTuber, deaf and disabled activist particularly known for her unique blend of entertaining and educational videos on vintage fashion, LGBTQ+ history, disability topics and identity. Her charming, warm and positive presentation style has not only seen her reach grow to over one million subscribers on YouTube and 400k followers on Instagram but has also won accolades, from an LGBT Brit Award to a place on the Shaw Disability Power 100 List. She lives in Brighton with her wife, toddler, dogs and many, many petticoats.

Elle McNicoll is a bestselling and award-winning novelist and screenwriter. Her debut middle grade novel, *A Kind of Spark*, won the Blue Peter Book Award and the Overall Waterstones Children's Book Prize, as well as Blackwell's Book of 2020. It was also adapted for television, was Emmy-nominated and won Best Children's Programme at the Broadcast Awards in London, 2024. She is now a four-time Carnegie-nominated author, and her YA debut, *Some Like It Cold*, is out now. She is an advocate for better representation of neurodiversity in publishing, and currently lives in North London. www.ellemcnicoll.com

Daniel Sluman is a poet and disability rights activist, with three poetry collections under his belt. His most recent, *Single Window*, was shortlisted for the T. S. Eliot Prize. One of a number of young poets who engaged with UK government cuts to disability benefits in the 2010s, Daniel co-edited anthology *Stairs and Whispers: D/deaf and Disabled Poets Write Back*, described as the first major UK disability anthology by disabled poets. Daniel's poems appear widely in UK poetry journals. He lives in Oxfordshire with his wife and their young son.

Nina Tame is a disability content creator, writer and mentor from the UK. With more than a hundred thousand followers on Instagram, she uses social media to discuss the way ableism works in her life and debunk outdated myths about disability. Her experience of growing up disabled herself, and now parenting a disabled child, run through her work. With wit, passion and lots of wheelchair selfies, Nina's work explores the nuances of the disabled experience while contributing to the growing, diverse and brilliant online disabled community. Find her @nina_tame.

Rebekah Taussig is a Kansas City writer who lives in a house full of half-finished art projects and loud music. She writes to understand, to reclaim and to participate in changing the cultural narratives we have around disability, motherhood and what it means to live in a human body. She is the author of the bestselling memoir *Sitting Pretty*, writes regularly on her Substack, This Too, and co-writes 'Roadmaps', a disability advice column. www.rebekahtaussig.com

Steven Verdile is a humour writer, designer and creator of *The Squeaky Wheel*, the first-ever satire publication focused on disability. Memorable articles include: 'Mediocre Disabled Employee Fails to Inspire Coworker' and 'Move Over, Disability Pride Month: It's White Wheelchair Guy Summer'. He lives in New York City with his girlfriend, spending his mornings drinking iced coffee and his evenings bingeing television and going to see musicals. He's a full-time wheelchair user with an avowed dislike of stairs.

Alex Wegman is a writer, storyteller, homeschooling mother of two, and lifelong wheelchair user. She tells stories, mainly on Instagram, about life at the intersection of disability and parenting, friendship, and generally existing in public. Alex has a degree in psychology, and sings in her spare time. She lives with her husband Bryan and their children Arwen and Asa in the Santa Cruz Mountains, USA.

Ashley Harris Whaley is a US writer, speaker, speech-language pathologist and disability activist. She's the creator of the Instagram account Disability Reframed, which focuses on changing perspectives through education and conversation, and Director of Adult Programs for the Cerebral Palsy Foundation. Ashley is a public speaker who educates on anti-ableism, disability identity, the language used around disability and allyship, and has written a children's book, *I Am, You Are: Let's Talk About Disability, Individuality and Empowerment.*

Kendra Winchester is a writer and podcaster. She is a contributing editor for Book Riot where she writes about audiobooks and disability literature; she is the editor for a forthcoming Appalachian disability anthology; and she is also the founder of Read Appalachia, which celebrates Appalachian literature and writing. Previously, Kendra co-founded and served as executive director for *Reading Women*, a podcast that gained an international following over its six-season run. In her off hours, you can find her writing on her Substack, Winchester Ave, and posting photos of her corgis on Instagram: @kdwinchester.